THE PAINTINGS OF RAUMA

A Jussi Alonen Detective Adventure

John Swallow

The characters and events portrayed in this book are fictitious. Any similarity to real persons, living or dead, is coincidental and not intended by the author.

ISBN-13: 9798653891243
ISBN-10: 1477123456

Cover design by: Art Painter
Library of Congress Control Number: 2018675309
Printed in the United States of America

CONTENTS

PROLOGUE

In 1885, Peter Carl Fabergé, a renowned jeweller, received an imperial commission from Tsar Alexander 3rd to design and produce an Easter egg for his bride Maria Feodorovna. Fabergé created an opaque white enamel egg with a gold yolk. Inside were some tiny surprises, including a hen and a replica of the imperial crown and pendant.

Subsequently, Fabergé received a commission from the Tsar to create a new egg to be presented every Easter. After the death of Alexander 3rd, the new Tsar, Nicholas II, continued to commission two eggs every year. One of these beautiful eggs was for his Tsarina, Alexandra Feodorovna and the other for his mother. Thus, a remarkable total of fifty Easter Eggs were created over the years.

However, in October 1917, the Bolsheviks seized power in Russia, and the Tsar and his family were later executed. The precious Fabergé eggs were subsequently confiscated. Some eggs were recovered; others may have been sold or stolen.

The hunt for the missing Fabergé Eggs still continues today.

INTRODUCTION

'Tervetuloa Raumalla!' (Finnish) - 'Welcome to Rauma!'

Rauma is an attractive city on the west coast of Finland. It was founded in 1442 within the county of Satakunta. It was designated a UNESCO world heritage site in 1991 due to its historically significant old town.

Old Rauma comprises over six hundred traditional wooden buildings, some of which are centuries old. Its picturesque buildings are covered in weathered wooden panels in a variety of colours. There are around eight hundred inhabitants, and the buildings host shops, cafes, museums and residences.

Rauma's commercial roots lie in shipbuilding and paper production. It is also well-known for traditional lace, celebrated by an annual festival: Pitsi Vikko (Lace Week). Rauma also has its own dialect of Finnish, called Rauman Giäl, still practised by some inhabitants. Aside from being a popular place to visit for Finns, Rauma's reputation as an international tourist destination continues to grow.

'Ol Niingon Gotonas!' (Rauma language) - 'Feel at Home!'

THE MUSEUM

It was freezing. Not just cold, but the kind of cold that chills your very bones. It was quiet as well, almost silent, save for the deliberate crunch of Jussi's boots on the snow-frosted pavement.

He turned the corner between two of the old town's main streets. From the snow-covered street of Savilankatu, he strode forward onto the snow-less street of Kuninkaankatu. The cobbles had been removed and replaced some years before, also rerouting the hot water pipes, resulting in this unusual change of scene.

Jussi strolled along the street, looking at shop windows and doors with familiar names, identifying each shop with its owners. He knew some of them well, as he had walked this street a thousand times before.

That evening, Jussi, together with his partner Harri, had driven around Rauma on a routine police patrol. They had been checking for the occasional Sunday evening speeder or perhaps even drunk driver, still merrily partying their way through the weekend.

The evening had been uneventful, though, aside from an abandoned, broken-down car, easily traced to its owner. It seemed that the law-abiding citizens of Rauma were either relaxing in their homes with the television or preparing for the week ahead with a relaxing sauna.

Jussi Alonen had experienced an undemanding but enjoyable career in the Police force so far. Four years had gone by quickly. During that time, he had learned most of the things he would ever need to police the city of Rauma. He was an ambitious man, but there seemed little opportunity for promotion locally. In Finland, many people remained in the same job or company for a long time, and it was the same in the police force. Senior officers were experienced and capable, with no reason to leave, and most would probably stay until retirement. To Jussi, it looked like a long road ahead to gain any kind of significant step-up in his career.

From time to time, Jussi considered moving to a bigger city for more opportunities. He could go to Turku? Tampere? or even Helsinki? Maybe his career could really take off in one of these places, and he could achieve his dream of becoming a detective. He didn't have many ties in Rauma, so such a move would be straightforward from a practical perspective. After a while, though, these thoughts usually faded away as he returned to day-to-day life in Rauma, the place he now called home.

Jussi had actually grown up in Eura, a small town about forty minutes away, on the banks of a large lake named Pyhäjärvi (Holy Lake). He had spent most of his youth in that area, then, following his military service, he had applied to the police force. Subsequently, his education had taken him to the city of Tampere to study at the police college.

After graduation, he jumped at the chance of a position in Rauma. He already knew the city quite well, and with Eura being close by, everything about his decision seemed to fit neatly into place.

Over the past couple of years, he hadn't revisited Eura much. His parents had passed away, and some of his friends had moved to bigger cities. Therefore, Jussi's visits to Eura usually took the form of occasional meetings with old school friends. These were good times and he enjoyed seeing them again. They would meet up for the group's annual Little Christmas Party or an occasional sauna evening, by the lake, in the summertime.

Jussi had settled well in Rauma. After initially renting for a year, he had bought a small but pleasant apartment in Old Rauma, the historic quarter of the city. It had everything he needed, which actually wasn't that much. The layout included a living room, kitchen, bedroom, small sauna, outside wooden terrace and a garage. It had been a good find as everything he needed was available within walking distance, although he had his car for longer trips when required.

Socially, he had made friends through work. This, combined with his growing allegiance to Lukko, the local ice hockey team, provided enough social interaction to be content. Also, Lukko had done rather well recently, making his investment of a season ticket a good one.

And his relationships? There had been a few. Jussi was a good prospect, at least in his opinion, with a promising career and income. However, he was already twenty-nine years old, and none of his relationships had worked out that well so far.

Once, he had almost been engaged; however, something about the situation hadn't felt quite right, so he had broken it off. He could have been married now, with a couple of children, a pleasant house and a station wagon. That life could have been okay, but no, not yet. Jussi still had many things he wanted to do in life and enjoyed his own space. Anyway, he might not have time for cross-country skiing, photography, and ice hockey matches if he had a family. She might also complain about his job; others had done that. Some didn't understand his career, but he wasn't prepared to change it for anyone. Many of his colleagues felt the same way. It was just the way things were in the force.

Kuninkaankatu wasn't such a long street to walk, from one

end to the other, but he had been taking his time that evening. He was alone with his thoughts and dawdled in front of the familiar camera store. He had been considering the purchase of a new camera for a while now. He was a keen photographer, although he thought himself keener than he actually was. His camera at home was a good one, but it spent most of its time in automatic mode.

In his apartment, he displayed an impressive amount of his own work on the walls. With the kind of scenery available in Finland, opportunities for exceptional photographs are easy to find. He enjoyed shooting in forests and lakes and especially the wildlife that inhabited them.

Jussi stopped and stood for a moment, looking around. He noted with interest that a shop had recently changed ownership, and new products were being displayed in the window. You couldn't miss such changes when the shop windows were so brightly lit against the dark evenings of a nordic winter.

He continued walking and reached the old town square. It looked stunning in the moonlit frost, with sparkling snow draping a surreal, shimmering blanket over the roofs of the old houses.

Soon they would begin with decorations for Christmas. It was nearing the end of November, and the enormous Christmas tree would spring up, festooned with lights. Spruce branches would appear over shop doorways, making every corner of the town appear like a traditional Christmas card. There was a thriving Christmas market in the town square too, with hot Glögi (a drink of local mulled berry juice and spirit) warming the hearts of the beaming clientele.

Jussi enjoyed Christmas in Rauma, and he reminded himself of its beauty every time he considered moving away. Of course, more prominent cities had their attractions in terms of career prospects and activities, but they didn't look quite like this.

I really must learn how to do more with my camera, Jussi reminded himself as he took in the view around him.

He suddenly shuddered as an icy chill blew through his coat.

Okay, that was a pleasant walk - but now I need to get home.

Hunger reminded him that the salmon soup he had made the day before would heat up in just a few minutes in the microwave.

The soup will be delicious washed down with a glass of of that wine, left over from the weekend, he decided.

Jussi enjoyed cooking, but he was sometimes tempted to eat the cereal bars he always had to hand, not just for snacking but sometimes as a complete replacement. Cooking for one was time-consuming, and snacking had become an easy solution, but not tonight. Right now, he needed something warm and filling.

He started along the remaining half of the street, now at a faster pace. His brain had decided he was getting colder and needed to eat and get warm as soon as possible; his legs responded accordingly. He expected to walk the remaining half a kilometre to his apartment in less than five minutes.

Let's make that a target, he decided as he glanced at his watch.

It was because of his current food-focused mindset that Jussi didn't react immediately to the oncoming situation. Later, he would tell his colleague, Harri, that everything seemed to happen in slow motion. 'How can sound happen in slow motion?' he had asked. But that's how it felt to him at that moment.

Smash!

It sounded as if a massive window had fallen onto the square and broken into a thousand pieces. The sound shattered the still of night and bounced off the surrounding buildings. After processing the noise for a couple of seconds, Jussi spun around to find out what had happened and where it had come from. By instinct, he walked quickly towards where he thought the source might be.

Was it there? No, further. Way over there? Could it be over there?

Although it felt as if he was being slow, his mind processed these questions in seconds as he made his way across the square.

Could the sound have come from the street near the museum? Even the museum itself?

There was no movement anywhere, except his own; no other noise nor broken glass was to be heard. It was still bright despite it being late at night, due to the square's lights illuminating the snow, and the sky being clear and starlit. He checked around once more without breathing, just in case he could pick something up from somewhere. He thought he heard another sound from the direction of the museum, and decided it was exactly where he needed to be.

Jussi saw nothing from the front and so walked around the side of the building down the small side street. He noticed a disturbance of snow on top of the gate, at the side entrance of the Museum yard. He jumped up and grabbed the top of it to gain a better view, pulling himself upwards. Committed to his decision, he scrambled over the wooden slats. He felt the old wood rip into his left hand as the splinters tore into his gloves. He cursed to himself as he managed to vault over the top of the gate and leap down into the darkness of the backyard.

He stood still for a moment. There was complete silence. He felt his way across the yard, steadying himself on objects as it was so dark, touching a post here and a wall there. He trod carefully so as not to make any noise. He quickly found the probable source of the smashing noise: the old half-glazed back door had a large jagged hole stretched across one of the glass panes, from corner to corner.

He pulled at the door, and it opened with a shudder; old wood which had expanded in the cold, damp air of winter. Some shards of glass fell away, and Jussi cursed under his breath at the sound of it hitting the icy stone step below. He was breathing heavier now, and the freezing, dry air seemed to catch his breath as he did so. He stared through the pitch blackness inside but could neither hear nor see anything, so he began to move, and felt his way slowly and gingerly through the hallway.

He shouted the prescribed warning, "Police! Show yourself!" Then demanded, "Where are you? This is the Police!"

Nothing again - it was still quiet.

He followed the passage, creeping carefully along the old wooden panels as he looked for a light switch. He cursed that he wasn't in uniform when he could have taken advantage of his clip-on torch to light his way. He would also have been grateful for the reassuring grip of his gun.

Finally, Jussi's fingers found a panel with a switch, and he flicked the control to illuminate the hallway. A dim light began to glow from a single ceiling lightbulb inside a small shade, as it gradually summoned the energy to illuminate the narrow space.

He walked with a purpose through the passage and across to another bank of lights. It was an old system for an old building, and Jussi flicked each switch. He shouted another warning, this time with more purpose and volume, then crept through an archway and made his way into the main gallery.

Now he knew where he was. He'd been in this part of the building several times before. After a brief scan around the space, he pulled out his phone and tapped in the police station number. After a single ring, the phone was answered, and he heard the desk officer's reassuring voice on the end of the line.

"Hello, Rauma Police?" Pekka answered.

"Pekka. Its Jussi. I'm at the town museum, on the square. There's been a break-in. I'm inside the building now. The suspects may still be in the area. Send backup."

Jussi's police training ensured that he provided the minimum information required to convey the importance of the message within the shortest time-frame possible.

"Just one moment, Jussi," Pekka disappeared for a moment and then returned to confirm, "They're on their way" and then asked, "What's your situation? Are you okay?"

"Everything's quiet here now. But I haven't checked everywhere yet."

"Wait for back-up, Jussi - you never know," advised Pekka.

Pekka was an experienced officer, nearing retirement, but still with a brain as sharp as a needle. He had the kind of voice that easily lent itself to listening. He always spoke with a calm level of knowledge and experience that everyone admired.

Jussi continued to hold the phone while his eyes darted around the room, watching for any sign of movement or danger.

Perhaps someone raided the cash register? Jussi thought to himself.

Although, he couldn’t think of a place in Rauma less likely to have money waiting inside the till drawer. The Museum was maintained by the town council, and the small donations and purchases from the gift shop would hardly make a smash-and-grab raid worthwhile. Besides, the building was so exposed on the central square that such a risk would be pointless.

He suddenly remembered the stairs and peered around the corner. Nothing seemed amiss, and everything was quiet until the welcome piercing sound of a police siren came into earshot. He heard cars scraping to a halt on the frozen cobbled stones outside.

Jussi pocketed the phone and made for the door. It was secured by a drop-latch and key, still in the lock. He waved the arriving officers forward, who were peering through the windows with torches, then beckoned them around to the side of the building while he ran back through the hallway.

His surroundings were now quite bright, and he felt better about every detail being visible. He saw a switch by the back door, flicked it on, and a lightbulb illuminated the small yard in a yellowish haze. He returned to the gate he had clambered over, to inspect it. He noted it was closed by a simple latch, so it couldn't be opened from the outside but not actually locked. He lifted the handle and swung the gate open.

That's not the most secure entrance, he surmised. *Then again, it's not exactly a bank.*

Jussi was met by two of his colleagues and his superior officer: Inspector Maarit Hänninen. Jussi smiled when he saw them. He noted another officer had remained at the front of the building, guarding the main door.

"What's the situation Jussi?" Maarit asked, her eyes surveying the yard.

As an experienced senior officer, she instantly commanded respect as someone who could take control of any given situation, without a second thought.

"I was on my way home when I heard a smash. The museum has been broken into by the back door. I didn't see anyone when I arrived, but I haven't had time to search yet," he replied.

"Okay, Tuomas, you stay here at the gate, and we'll check the building. Jussi, come with us," Maarit directed.

The two officers in front began to walk through the passageway. They moved slowly and deliberately through the building, step by step, initially around the first floor and then the upstairs.

"Jussi, track down the keyholders and call them in," directed Maarit.

"Will do."

Jussi knew the manager and some of the staff at the museum. He pulled out his mobile phone to make the calls. While he was doing so, other officers checked every cupboard, door and corner of the building. They found nothing except the flashing reflection of blue and white lights from the police vehicles outside.

Maarit barked orders into her phone again. She directed another car to drive around the area to look for anyone acting suspiciously.

Half an hour later, Heidi, the museum manager, appeared at the door of the museum. On hearing the news, she had dropped her knitting and abandoned her planned evening of television. After the call from Jussi, Heidi had carefully covered herself in knitted clothing layers, and made her way over to her place of work. She wore a worried demeanour. This kind of thing did not happen in Rauma.

Discussions commenced within the assembled group about the Why? What? and How? of the crime. Firstly, what kind of crime was it?

A window had been broken, and someone seemed to have entered the property, presumably with malicious intent. However, nothing appeared to have been taken or damaged deliberately, except the door. Perhaps it could just have been an act of vandalism by some bored teenagers? Although, this was rare in the town and would be a step beyond the usual incidents.

Could it have been an opportunist thief, made braver by the combination of alcohol, a quiet night and an easy target? Afterall, who would plan to break into this old place? Thoughts were exchanged, but to all intents and purposes, that was that.

At 12.30 am, almost exactly an hour from when Jussi had heard the noise, the episode was over. The police arranged a locksmith to temporarily secure the back door and window, while guarding the building. At the same time, another officer arrived to check the area for fingerprints and other potentially valuable evidence of the crime. Although, in this weather, it was likely that gloves had been worn anyway, they surmised. In addition, notes and photographs were taken for the crime report.

Jussi strolled around the museum one last time and cast his eyes into every nook and cranny. The interior of the building reflected the beauty of the outside. It was old, made mainly of wood, with cornices and carvings reflecting its past. Hardly anything had been changed over the years due to preservation laws, and Rauma was thankful for this. History was rapidly disappearing worldwide, and the city took real pride that Old Rauma was being preserved.

Well, probably that's all there is to it, he decided.

Now the building had been checked and secured, it was time to go home. Jussi was already planning to make a quick visit in the morning as a courtesy to make sure everything was alright. He knew Heidi, the manager, quite well, and although it might not become his case, he still felt some responsibility. After he finished walking around the building, Maarit made a beeline for him.

"Good work, Jussi! Quick thinking. Lucky you were in the area. Maybe it was someone from out of town who thought there were valuable antiques here? There aren't any, though. Also, the cash register is untouched, and nothing has been taken - you probably scared the suspect away!" She congratulated him and then added, "Heidi, I think we should call it a night now. We'll leave a patrol car outside for an hour, and they'll check the area a few times during the night, but I don't expect any further incidents. We'll check in with you in the morning. In addition to fixing the door, I suggest you ask the locksmith to secure that back gate with a deadlock and an extra bolt. Perhaps it may deter another opportunist in future?"

Heidi flinched a little at the Inspector's view of the value of the items within the museum. In her opinion, there were indeed valuable antiques here. In reality, though, most of them were only significant to the city of Rauma. They were also important to her personally, as she regarded herself as the guardian of this little piece of history.

At this point, Jussi began to think out loud.

"Why make all of the effort to scale the wall and break in without stealing anything? If this was a vandal or a passing drunk, surely there are easier targets?"

He scanned the walls and shelves once more in the hope of a secret revealing itself to him - it didn't.

Shortly afterwards, he decided his work was over, expressed sympathy to Heidi again, said good-bye to his colleagues, and made for the door. He was drained now, and despite the hour, he was also famished.

Suddenly, he saw it, on his way out of the museum. He glanced upwards, and just above the door, noticed a painting that had settled diagonally at its corner on the narrow shelf above the door. Every other picture and photograph was positioned squarely on the wall. His eyes darted around the room - everything else was perfectly and neatly arranged. By the look of it, they had been like that for decades.

Could this be something?" he thought.

"Heidi?" he asked slowly.

Heidi was currently repositioning some items on the reception desk.

"Yes?" she answered equally slowly, without raising her head from the task.

"Is there something wrong up there?"

"Where?" Heidi asked.

"Up there, above the door. That painting of the field of yellow crops. Has it always been in that position, with the corner resting on the shelf?"

"Oh no, dear," she replied. "It's always attached to the wall further above; it must have fallen. Oh, wait a moment, that's not the painting that normally hangs there. It has always been the painting of the old Sali, now the Café. It was painted in front of the museum, with the view right across the square. It's been here for many years now. I leave it there to show people how the view across the square has changed so little over the years."

"Do you remember moving it? Or could any of your staff have changed it?"

"No, I don't, and no - nobody would dare. I'm very precise about what is hanging on my walls. I talk about that view every day, and would have known if anything had changed."

"Okay, I'd just like to check something. It's a little too high. Do you have a ladder? " Jussi asked, straining on his toes to get a good view of the shelf.

"There's a set of steps at the back, in the recess."

She gestured over to the hallway. It was the one through which Jussi had already walked twice that night.

"Be careful please, they are rather old. I keep thinking of getting new ones but we don't make so much in our till these days, and our budget is quite tight."

Jussi found the step-ladders tucked away in a corner and

brought them, rattling, to the front of the store. He opened the steps and stepped up to the fifth rung.

Now, he had a good view of the area in question. Sure enough, the painting was perched precariously with its corner on the shelf.

Slipping on gloves from his pocket and confirming that it was not attached in any way, he carefully removed the painting. He stepped off the ladder and placed the picture on the reception desk, warning that it shouldn't be touched until dusted for fingerprints.

Jussi made his way up the steps once more and noted that the dust had been disturbed. Luckily, the area wasn't tended to so often, being higher up. It was easy to see an image of where a painting had previously sat for some time, as the same shape and size had discoloured the paint. Glancing downwards, he could see the yellowish area was smaller than the larger painting currently occupying the reception desk. Clearly, a picture had previously been moved or removed.

He relayed his findings to the waiting audience below, who by this point consisted of Heidi, Maarit and two of his colleagues. They were all eager to know what Jussi had discovered. They were in no particular rush either and were enjoying the warmth inside. Heidi had also mentioned the possibility of coffee, so there was plenty of time to indulge Jussi's investigation.

About the painting, Heidi confirmed that it had indeed been in place the previous day. She assured everyone that she would check with her staff in the morning. She would ascertain if anyone, woe betide them, had moved the picture from its designated position.

Jussi thanked her, placed the painting carefully back into position, and removed the step ladder. He also gave instructions that everything should be left as it was until the results of

Heidi's research were received.

Heidi's face, now portrayed a mixture of annoyance and excitement. She was annoyed due to the possible movement or loss of a painting but relished her new role as an amateur sleuth.

Jussi, once again said his goodbyes, and finally a little after 1 am, left for home.

The temperature hadn't improved outside, and the increasingly chilly wind kept his wits razor-sharp as he walked, even faster this time. His ears and eyes were on full alert, lest some other form of theft or vandalism was occurring somewhere else. Thankfully, nothing else happened.

Finally, at 1.20 am, Jussi entered his apartment. He heated his long-awaited salmon soup in the microwave and ate it together with a glass of water instead of wine. Then, he brushed his teeth and turned in.

It had been a long day. As he lay in bed, his mind turned over for some minutes. He was far too tired to think about the events of the night for too long, though, and soon fell sound asleep.

A MYSTERY

The cafe on the square swung into action at 8.00 am, and the early rush of locals began to gather around the counter. There were a few bursts of activity during the day; lunchtime was always the peak time, but opening in the morning also brought a small queue. These early customers were keen to dive into their first coffee of the day, sometimes accompanied by a fresh pulla (cinnamon bun), before heading off towards work for whatever the day had in store.

Despite his short night, Jussi had been awake since 6.30 am and was still hungry from his nocturnal activities. With little in the fridge, he was among the first customers at the cafe, eager for fresh coffee. Having smelled the delicious aroma in the building on arrival, he also decided on a large warm pulla. In Jussi's opinion, the smell of coffee and fresh pulla on an icy-cold morning was one of the best smells in Finland and almost irresistible.

He flashed a customary smile at the counter.

"Hyvää Huomenta" (Good Morning) and ordered his breakfast.

As he ate, he casually observed the characters around the café. There was the usual assortment of local store owners, market stallholders and a few people he didn't recognise.

Tourists maybe? he thought to himself, observing a small group. *Perhaps having a day trip from Helsinki.*

In fact, Rauma was experiencing a growing number of tourists who flocked to see the medieval buildings, narrow streets, and unspoiled beauty of its old town. This was especially true in summer when the number of boats on the harbour almost doubled. Visitors came from Germany, Sweden, Norway and beyond. Throughout history, Rauma citizens have been seafaring people, and boat ownership is common.

Jussi smiled as he remembered a comment he had heard many times before:

Rauma folk are seafaring people, and if told that someone had passed away, a person would express sympathy, and then casually ask what kind of boat they had owned.

Helsinki, the capital city of Finland, was rapidly becoming an airline hub for the far east. Many Asian visitors were exploring Finland every year to see its historic buildings, northern lights, and scenic countryside. Technology and nuclear power also attracted workers from overseas; some made it as far as Rauma. This influx of tourists, sometimes arriving by bus from the capital, was welcomed by local retailers, restaurants and cafes. They provided a welcome boost to local finances.

Jussi's shift didn't start until 4 pm, so apart from the short nap he was planning to have to recover from the night before, he had time to spend on personal matters. He had a list in his pocket, as was often his habit, written on a sticky note from his fridge door. It contained the usual essentials he would need to get by over the next few days: milk, bread, cheese, muesli, cereal bars and coffee. His daily diet was quite basic unless he had guests, when he would grab his cookbooks and play chef with more exotic ingredients. He was quite accomplished in this regard and usually turned out something impressive. However, his preference in the summertime was simply to throw a steak or some sausages onto the barbeque, accompanied by a few cold beers.

He was sitting at a table by the window of the café - his

favourite spot in the mornings. He watched with interest as the museum began to open for the day. As he did so, his mind returned to the events of the previous night. His list for the supermarket evaporated as he decided he must find out if the puzzle of the painting was indeed a mystery or simply a memory lapse of Heidi, the museum manager. He knew there would be an investigation, but he still owed it to her to show interest and support even if he wasn't involved.

He decided to visit the museum, so after systematically donning his layers, he was ready for the cold outside. After giving the girls behind the counter a wave, he strode purposefully across the square's cobblestones.

It was 8.40 am, and the first glimmers of sunshine were rising from above the buildings. Immediately, he was waved down by the growing group of senior citizens gathered around the coffee kiosk. Jussi was also known to frequent this place, known for its hot coffee and local information.

"Moro (Hello) Jussi, so what happened last night then?" Two of the men asked almost simultaneously.

As always, news had travelled fast and there was nowhere faster than between its senior citizen's - Rauma's very own human intranet.

"We don't know yet as we haven't concluded our investigation," Jussi answered with a smile.

"Hah," one said, "I heard it was a break-in; maybe someone stole an antique or painting? Was it valuable?"

Jussi cringed at the questions and wondered how many people were already discussing this over coffee that morning, pondering their own theories. By lunchtime, these would be stretched out of all proportion.

Rauma was a small city with little crime. Something like this certainly had the makings of a big story in the local newspaper. From experience, he knew he had to guard his words carefully.

"You can be sure I'll inform you in due course," Jussi clipped, accompanied by a wink.

With that, he beat a hasty retreat from the gathering crowd. One of the perils of being a police officer was never really being off duty. Jussi knew he had to be especially aware of his remarks at all times. Even a tiny inflexion or facial expression could discharge a whole new rumour, scattering varying and exaggerated versions of the truth across surrounding farms and villages. A topic like this could quickly become the day's coffee-break topic of choice.

Jussi arrived at the museum and, noticing Heidi inside, rapped on the door. She hadn't unlocked everything yet but made straight for the door to let him in. Before he was able to open his mouth in greeting, she was already blurting out her news.

"It was there. The painting. I checked with everyone. It was there yesterday. Someone stole it! Why would they do that? It wasn't worth much at all, except to Rauma."

This was the news that Jussi had been expecting and looking forward to hearing. Now, perhaps he could make some sense of what had happened. He settled in with a proffered mug of steaming hot, black coffee, declining milk and sugar, and took out his notebook to write down the details.

After an exciting and rather animated discussion with Heidi, Jussi summarised the facts in his notebook:

Break-in at 11.33 am at the old town museum; Window of the back door damaged to gain entry; One missing painting confirmed; Nothing else apparently taken; No suspects identified or detained; Building secured and repair arrangements made; Further research required to determine the value of the stolen item:

Motive unknown; Crime number issued for insurance purposes.

Although he couldn't say for sure at this stage, he was doubtful if any more evidence would turn up now, such as fingerprints or tools used in the crime. Of course, the prescribed checks and investigations would be done, but unless they found the painting nearby, it was probably gone for good.

It would also later be reported that CCTV footage from cameras overlooking the square couldn't identify anything. Anyway, no cameras were pointed directly at the museum, from either the front or the rear.

Perhaps the CCTV will need to be changed in future? Jussi questioned. *Then again, the value of the artefacts inside and the difficulty of selling them might not justify it.*

Following the incident, locks were changed, photographs taken, and statements made. Extra patrols were scheduled to monitor activities on the square over the following weeks as a precautionary measure. An Officer would even occasionally check and rattle the door and gate to ensure they had not been tampered with. That was all the police could do at this stage.

The rest of the day passed as usual, without anything of note. Jussi had completed his shopping trip for essentials and made arrangements for the forthcoming weekend.

At 4 pm, he arrived at the police station and started his detective work. He had already telephoned and requested to process the case, approval of which had been granted. This work would comprise: completing the case notes, checking the missing and stolen websites, updating information about the painting from the museum's inventory, and general research on the internet to find additional information. It was still essential to build a complete case file for future reference, even if they didn't solve the crime.

On reading the museum inventory, it listed as follows:

Painting of Rauma town square and surrounding buildings; Painted in 1910 by Stefan Hämäläinen; Sold by a local art store in Rauma to a private customer; Item given to the museum as a gift in 1950; No official appraised valuation but current value estimated at 600€; Currently part of the Vanha Rauma Museum collection.

Perhaps the intruder had taken a liking to the painting and intended to take it, in addition to other valuables? Maybe they mistook the picture's value, and that was all that could be removed in the short time before being disturbed?

He summarised the facts and noted that it was probably an isolated event with no specific motive. He recommended increasing security at the museum and submitted his report.

Jussi's superiors agreed that all was in order. The 'action taken' section was completed, and he sent a copy of the police report to the museum for insurance purposes. Then, he made arrangements for a regular police presence over the next four weeks. The case was marked as open and awaited any further developments.

FIRST BLOOD

Monday morning arrived after a busy weekend for Jussi. On Friday evening, he had enjoyed an excellent sauna evening with friends, accompanied by plenty of beer and grilled sausages. On Saturday, he had managed a workout in the gym, after which his local ice hockey team, Lukko, had beaten their closest rivals to move up a place in the league. Finally, on Sunday, he had relaxed, walked in the forest and taken some photographs. The weekend had ended with a movie night.

Not a bad way to spend a weekend off, he considered.

In addition to all the activity, he had received a surprise phone call from an old friend. Her name was Heli, and she now lived in London. She had suggested they should meet as she would visit Helsinki soon on business. She had been a previous romantic interest of Jussi's, whom he remembered fondly.During the period in his life when they had been close, they couldn't decide whether they were friends or lovers and had agreed to part ways and explore their own lives. Her call had come entirely out of the blue, and he'd been thrilled to receive it.

For this reason, Jussi had a spring in his step on this Monday morning, even though his shift would start at 7 am.

With a fridge now full of food for a change, he had breakfast at home, slipped a pack of his favourite cereal bars into his backpack and walked briskly along his preferred route through town.

Jussi owned a car, but he preferred to walk everywhere when

in town, only using his car for longer excursions. He had a second-hand black, jeep-type vehicle in good condition. This suited his purpose and had been reliable over the years. Also, it was in great shape and had less than 50,000 kilometres on the dial - primarily because it spent its time under cover of his garage.

Looking outside, he saw the snow had fallen heavily during the night, as much as fifteen centimetres in some places. The snowploughs and tractors had been toughing it out since the early morning. Luckily, Jussi's apartment needed very little work to maintain a path through the winter snow due to its sunny southerly aspect. Also, thanks to the underground heating system under the streets, the central streets in Rauma were relatively clear. As always, this gave the old town a surreal atmosphere, as if it had been lifted out of Finland, had the snow shaken off it and neatly put back in place again.

Jussi appreciated the view as he strode along, in his light but warm, casual clothes. It was still dark that morning, but with the Christmas lights illuminating the windows and the snow layered over the roofs, it couldn't have looked more festive.

Christmas is on its way, thought Jussi.

He resolved to begin Christmas shopping the very next weekend to avoid his traditional last-minute rush around the crowded stores. He liked to consider himself organised, but there were exceptions, and shopping was, without doubt, the biggest of those. He preferred to complete his Christmas shopping list in Rauma, where possible, and buy anything else online. He chose to avoid the large commercial shopping centres in the bigger cities.

He strode down the main street, passing only a few people. Everyone seemed to have their heads buried in their scarves, looking downwards.

Perhaps they're all looking forward to their next steaming hot cup of coffee, he thought to himself.

Jussi took his usual route to the police station. He walked over the zebra crossing and down the avenue. Then, he cut through the small carpark in front of the restaurants. From there, he zig-zagged down the couple of streets that connected with the station.

He arrived at precisely 6.30 am, with a pleasant 'Hyvää Huomenta' (Good Morning) to Petri, the day's desk officer, before going to the locker room to change into his uniform.

Topias, one of his colleagues, was cradling a cup of coffee and reading the computer in front of him, apparently wholly lost in thought. Jussi's morning greeting jolted him into reality. After the automatic reaction of reciprocating, he blurted out the news on his mind.

"Have you heard what's happened?"

"No, something new?" Jussi questioned curiously.

"You might say that. Someone's been murdered - out at Urjala! The body was found this morning in a barn."

"What? Tell me more!"

As Jussi took a seat, he encouraged him to continue.

"Go ahead, I have time."

"The guys are out there already, and there's a forensics team on the way from Pori. I don't think the case will come our way, but this is the story so far."

Topias drew a deep breath and began his narration in a solemn and deliberate voice.

"Well, the old man owned a farm in the village of Urjala. He was retired and lived alone. One of his friends called by this morning to take him into town, but there was no answer, and the door was unlocked. The house was a real mess, with furniture overturned and everything all over the floor. His friend took a look around the place and eventually found him lying dead in the old barn."

Topias paused for both breath and effect.

"We don't know the cause of death, but it's being treated as suspicious due to the obvious break-in. There was so much blood everywhere too. They've also found a suspected murder weapon on the premises."

He finished the story with a flourish.

"So, not such a quiet night, again?" Jussi replied, "I can't remember the last time when there was a suspicious death. Well, Harri and I have our patrol first thing, so why don't we swing around there on our way and see if our assistance is needed? Let the desk sergeant know, would you."

"No problem, Jussi. See you later!" agreed Topias.

Jussi made his way to his desk to retrieve some equipment. While doing so, he bumped into his colleague Harri, who was already making his way through coffee number three.

"Come on, Harri," Jussi hustled. "Let's get on the road and swing by the murder scene."

"I don't think it's a murder scene yet, young man! I hear that it's just a suspicious death at this stage. Let me prepare some refreshments, and we'll soon be on our way."

Harri poured a large quantity of hot coffee from the jug into a flask and screwed on the lid. Jussi was not a massive fan of the bitter, amber-coloured liquid that Harri called coffee. He preferred a strong cappuccino from his favourite coffee shop or his machine at home. Still, there were times when Harri's coffee was a lifesaver, so he was grateful for his friend's habit.

Shortly afterwards, their police car swung out of the station, and its cabin gradually began to warm up. It was usually pot luck which cars made it into the garage, having space for only a few vehicles; the remaining ones being left outside. This time they were unlucky, and it made a quantifiable difference on such a chilly morning. Jussi could still see his breath as he tried to relax in the passenger seat. Even booting up the onboard computer, seemed slow, perhaps protesting the extreme cold.

Firstly, they drove into the old town, checking on the morning preparations underway for the city to awaken. They slowed down in front of the museum and sat there for a moment, taking in the events around them. Jussi knew Heidi would still be worried after the break-in. He wanted to show a regular police presence to restore her confidence and that of other local store owners. He was happy there had been no further issues in the town centre over the past days, although he hadn't expected there to be any.

After this, the car swung out of the square and drove out of the old town towards the docks. They continued onwards to the old railway station and then back towards the big supermarkets.

There were more cars than usual, with the supermarkets competing for Christmas shoppers. They were currently trying hard to outdo each other with unmissable offers for the festive season, which today would be washed down by free glögi. The next stop would be the school and then northward towards the Kaaro area.

After passing the school with its usual variety of bicycles, mopeds and mini-SUVs, Jussi steered the car past Kaaro and towards Urjala. Their planned schedule for the day was to drive a couple of circuits and then set up a speed checkpoint near the newer industrial area in Isometsä (Big Forest).

Some cars went at sixty km/hour there, in what was a fifty

km/hour zone. It was clearly breaking the law, but Jussi focused only on those determined to exceed the speed limit rather than those who hadn't noticed their speedometers by a few ticks. It was the police's job to apply the law in a fair and reasonable manner, and it was this way of thinking that had earned Jussi considerable respect in the area. He had, more often than not, made use of a warning rather than jumping straight to the stage of an on-the-spot fine.

They drove along the main road now, at a sedentary eighty km/hour, with the speed limit in Finland having been dropped by twenty km/hour in the winter for safety.

After leaving the town well behind, they soon came across the sign to Urjala.

Topias had been clear with his directions, and although Jussi knew the area well, he'd never turned onto the particular track on which they now found themselves. It had been cleared, but the snow was falling faster and covering it once again.

They jolted around the bumps and potholes as they went. Jussi wondered if there was still any evidence outside, as it must by now be hard to detect as the snow continued to fall. Eventually, an old farmhouse appeared at the end of the track in bright ochre, amongst flashing blue and white lights.

It was an old building, that despite looking as if it had seen better days seemed to have been recently repainted. It stood like a beacon against the snow-white landscape, with a selection of dilapidated buildings surrounding it.

They swung into the yard behind another police vehicle and jumped out - more Jussi's action, as Harri levered himself out of the cabin at a somewhat slower pace. This morning, he didn't share quite the same enthusiasm as his younger counterpart.

Walking towards the house, Jussi noted the surroundings in his head: the farmhouse, wood shelter, nearby barn, and further away: an old grain store that looked as if it was about to sink into the ground, being in poor condition.

A figure in regulation blue appeared in the doorway of the house.

"Hello Jussi, how are you?" Pekka asked.

He was genuinely pleased to see the young officer, but at the same time, slightly surprised that he was there.

"I'm fine, thanks and you?" replied Jussi.

"All good with me, but this is a sad case indeed."

"Yes, I heard. We thought we would swing by to see if we could help. So, what happened?"

"Well, it's pretty clear now that the old chap, Stefan Hämäläinen, already identified by his sister, was murdered here at his home last night. Forensics have already been all over the place and say they have found what appears to be the murder weapon - an old axe!"

"Why was he murdered? What was the motive? any ideas?"

"Nobody knows. It seems he was a quiet, unassuming old chap. He went downtown every couple of weeks with his sister and did some shopping, but apart from that, he stayed here and painted, quite profusely as it seems. There are hundreds of paintings stacked up all over the place, some going damp and mouldy."

Pekka shook his head and continued.

"The strange thing is that the pictures have been thrown around everywhere as if some psycho killed him and then took their anger out on his paintings as well. Not just here in the house but the barn too."

"That's odd," commented Harri.

Jussi asked, "What was his name again?"

"Stefan Hämäläinen. It's truly a bad business. Nobody deserves this. Poor old guy."

Jussi recognised the name and began raking his brain for more information. Then, he remembered.

"Stefan Hämäläinen was the name of the artist who did the painting that was stolen from the museum on Sunday evening."

They looked at each other, as Jussi rolled the question around in his head for a few moments.

The question that they were all asking themselves at that particular moment was:

What connection could there be between a stolen painting from a museum and the murder of the same artist and the ransacking of his home? - in the same area, within a few days of each other?

With the arrival of these thoughts, the snow suddenly reacted with new energy. It pushed them all towards the relative shelter of the house.

As there wasn't anything for Harri and Jussi to do there, they shared a swift coffee from Harri's flask and departed to their appointed tasks.

After their patrol, Jussi and Harri parked in a small layby, set back into the forest to hide the car, as they checked the speed of the sparse oncoming traffic. As they did so, they discussed the mysterious connection between the two recent events. They had already come up with a few theories and had settled on one for discussion.

Jussi began, "It would make sense for the two events to be

connected in some way, but I don't understand why someone would go after more of this man's paintings and kill him for them - if that was the idea? It wasn't as if his paintings were particularly good or valuable; worth just a few hundred euros, even if you could even find someone to buy them?"

"Or is there some other reason?" Harri asked. "Maybe someone didn't like the paintings, or he copied someone else's ideas, or he just hated his paintings, wanted to destroy them and then committed suicide?"

Jussi threw out these theories and regarded Harri with a painful expression.

"I can't say I agree with you, Harri, but I can't say that I can think of a motive myself either."

Later at the station, Jussi would learn that nothing visible had been taken from the farm. It was now officially a murder case, pending completion of the forensic tests over the next few days. He wasn't on the investigating team but naturally wanted to know more about the events, especially given the possible connection of the paintings.

But murder? It was decades since there'd been a murder in Rauma.

Once, Jussi had heard something about a jealous habitual drunkard with a shotgun and a bottle of vodka, but that was it. Well, time would tell. This was not his investigation, and maybe the two incidents were unconnected. Perhaps the whole thing had just been a coincidence?

When Jussi arrived home, he was happy to close the door and eat his takeaway from the local Thai restaurant. He had ordered his favourite meal of chicken and rice and decided to retire to bed early after that.

The day seemed to have been quite wearing somehow. Speed

check days were always quite challenging as they involved so much sitting around without much activity. Jussi was an action-orientated person and struggled with these assignments.

Shortly afterwards, after a brief scan of his tablet computer, he was happy to fade off to sleep and be energised for another day.

◆ ◆ ◆

Bzzzt! Bzzzt!

The phone yelled out suddenly.

Jussi awoke, jumping up suddenly at the sound of the call. He grabbed at his phone resting by the bed, missed it once, felt contact with it again and answered with a sleepy, hoarse voice.

"Hello, who is it?"

"Time to go," said the voice.

It was Harri on the other end of the line. Jussi noticed the time on his mobile phone - not even 4 am yet.

"What's up?"

"We need to go. There's been another break-in, and almost everyone else has already been called to an RTA (road traffic accident) near Pyhäräntä. The boss wants a car on the road to check the break-in, secure it and be visible around town."

"Okay, can you pick me up on the way?"

"Almost at your doorstep already, sleeping beauty. Rise and shine!"

Harri lived close to the police station, in an apartment overlooking the car park, so he'd been able to drop into the station and dive into the car within minutes.

Jussi quickly dressed, got ready and left the house, grabbing a cereal bar on his way. Coffee would've been good at this point, but as much as Harri loved his coffee, he wouldn't have put its preparation above an emergency call.

Blue and white lights were already flashing in front of Jussi's apartment, and he dived in through the passenger door. The car took off and briefly skidded, cutting through the icy ground with its metal studded tyres, making good progress along the street.

"Where are we going?" Jussi asked, regarding the car's GPS through heavy eyes.

"Back to the museum," Harri replied.

"Really? Has there been another break-in?" Jussi asked incredulously.

In Jussi's memory, the building had never been broken into. For it to happen twice in one week seemed nothing short of senseless. Also, the building had been secured with new locks and given regular police patrols. He secretly hoped Heidi had actually arranged the extra security, as it may otherwise cause him some criticism from Maarit, his superior.

As they pulled up at the museum, Jussi started to speculate if the highway accident had been designed as a diversion. No, he dismissed it from his mind as ridiculous. It would be way too much trouble to go to for this. Perhaps if there'd been a bank robbery or something like that, it would make sense, but not a break-in at the old museum.

They climbed out of the car into the night. Jussi felt the cold immediately, as he hadn't had time to dress appropriately. However, he had donned his spare uniform, which all police officers retain at home, that provided some protection against the elements. They arrived at the scene a few minutes later.

This time there'd been even less subtlety in the crime. The door had just been smashed in at one hinge by something powerful, then left sagging and creaking by the remaining one.

Jussi went inside quickly and looked around the familiar front space. Harri joined him, and the museum was again lit by their car's headlights and flashing blue lights, bouncing off every reflective surface.

Together, they slowly and deliberately made their way through the building; Again, there was no thief and, this time, no apparent sign of disturbance except the damaged doorway. Jussi clearly remembered the layout, and they could make their way through every room and darkened corner at speed.

After they had thoroughly checked the building, they regrouped by the door. There had been no rear door exit, and the perpetrator had almost certainly walked out of the front door.

"Who raised the alarm?" Jussi asked Harri.

"A lady who lives just across the street. It seems that she saw the front door partly open while walking her dog. We can check tomorrow if anyone in the area heard or saw anything else."

"I'll call Heidi, the manager, again," said Jussi. "Would you call the locksmith to secure the door somehow?" he asked, regarding the latest mess with disappointment.

With both feeling a distinct sense of déjà vu, the officers went through precisely the same process as before. They secured the building, then called and waited for both Heidi and the locksmith.

At Heidi's arrival, they discussed the repeated event with her. This time, she and Jussi went through the museum with a fine tooth-comb and nothing, but nothing evaded their eyes.

After the search, Jussi called the station and summarised the situation:

"We are as certain as we can be that nothing has been taken. We thought that last time, though, and later found that a painting had disappeared...yes, but we have checked and double-checked; it seems there is nothing else missing, at least not a painting this time....they didn't have any more of his paintings here, so that couldn't have been the motive. This keeps getting weirder, but there has to be a reason; we just need to find it. In the meantime, I will contact the city government in the morning and support Heidi with a request to fit a modern alarm linked to our system."

Shortly afterwards, Jussi was relieved from duty and was happy to find that his shift would be postponed that day. Therefore, he could sink back into his pillow once more. He was tired and cold.

Once more, Jussi went to bed almost as soon as he walked into his apartment and fell into a deep sleep - possibly dreaming of museums, broken doors and stolen paintings.

After a while, the strange events concerning the paintings, in and around Rauma, came to an end. Jussi's job returned to monitoring speed limits and attending occasional car accidents in the darkness of winter.

The following weeks passed with no museum break-ins and no more talk of stolen paintings. News in Rauma returned to normal and concentrated on more festive events ahead.

THE KIASMA

Helsinki is an impressive and picturesque capital city. It is small in population - about half a million people, and also in its geographical size. Almost everything of note can be found within a twenty-minute walk in any given direction from its geometric middle.

In the city centre, impressive buildings from the romantic Art Nouveau and Jugend eras gradually give way to more modern structures. These eventually evolve into a ubiquitous selection of modern Nordic apartment blocks.

Some might say traffic is heavy sometimes, but this is because the centre is small and the roadworks prolific. Anyone who has encountered severe traffic in other parts of the world would say it is a pleasure to drive or walk here. The only real but necessary annoyance is the constant state of building and road repairs. Like many cities these days, construction of some kind seems to be everywhere.

This particular Helsinki day was grey, really grey. The whole city was enveloped in a sea of monochrome, covering both buildings and people in a thick haze. The ground was a mixture of snow and hard crispy ice, with the temperature having dropped to minus twelve degrees. However, it felt even colder due to the blustery winds, which blew straight through clothes to the skin. People scurried around like mice, covered in their warmest clothes and with virtually no exposed skin visible to the elements.

The Kiasma modern art museum is in the centre of the city. It is an architectural triumph of jagged white walls and glass, seemingly half-sunk into the ground. Some might describe it as otherwise, but it is impressive nonetheless. It houses an ever-changing display of works from various artists in a suitably artistic setting. It also has a ground-level cafe and galleries positioned upwards and downwards via its white, winding staircase.

On winter days, it's possible to spend at least a couple of hours in the building. For tourists, it's a must-see destination, made all the more attractive due to its heating system.

During the afternoon, a curious thing happened inside the building, an event that would only be noted within the daily security report of the museum. No doubt, it would pass without further comment.

Someone had been taking a video of the paintings. Not just with a camera phone, as many tourists did, even when asked not to do so, but methodically and systematically, with a professional camera. A security guard had noticed it on one of the monitors and relayed this to a guard on patrol. There was no grave infraction being committed. However, it was the way the person was behaving. It was just odd and somewhat suspicious.

The guard in the control room had his full attention captured by the person's activities. With the network of security cameras around the building, it was possible to follow someone around the gallery, although there were several blind spots.

As he watched, he saw the man step over a security rope and walk over to a painting. The man proceeded to touch and examine the picture, feeling around the frame.

Filming was one thing, but this was quite another; this was certainly not allowed. The guard rose from his seat and talked into his radio. The patrolling guard, receiving the message, walked rapidly towards the area. However, when he arrived, the suspicious man was nowhere to be seen.

Back in the control room, the guard didn't see the man on any other monitors. How he had evaded the remaining cameras was quite odd.

After examination of the painting in question, the guards concluded that there had been no damage done. The man had just been touching it for some reason.

As for its value? It was part of a random mix of traditional winter landscape paintings from around Finland. The exhibit was primarily for tourists at this time of year. They would usually display more contemporary art pieces in that space.

The description noted for the daily report was that the person was a short, portly man wearing a dark coat, scarf and black cap. Of course, with these clothes, it left little to go on. The description would fit many people currently walking in and around the city centre, wrapped in their layers of dark clothing.

Over their coffee break, the guards lamented to each other why people wouldn't follow the gallery's rules. Why couldn't they just take a few photographs with their phones? - nobody minded that.

"Why would someone want to touch one of the paintings? What do they get out of that?" they asked each other, shaking their heads.

Then a couple of hours later, it was the end of their shift.

The man wasn't seen again, and nothing further occurred. The guards gave themselves some comfort in that the strange incident had momentarily broken the boredom of the day; they thought nothing more about it.

Indeed, after the unknown photographer's task had been completed, he had simply pulled up his scarf, pushed down his hat and melted away into the crowd outside.

And that, or so it seemed, was that.

CHILLING NEWS

Nothing further arose as a result of the Urjala murder investigation. Everything had been documented and photographed, but there was nothing else to do. The investigating officer had concluded that the file should remain open as an unsolved case. Events related to the sale of paintings, especially by the dead painter, Stefan Hämäläinen, within a 200 km radius of the murder, would be reviewed for similarities. The file was marked 'no further action at this time,' and the case was held in suspension, waiting for some discovery to bring it back to life.

After a few weeks, that is precisely what happened.

Närpiö or Närpes, also called, is a picturesque town about two hundred kilometres north of Rauma. This small, friendly town has an equally small attractive high street adjacent to a river and an old bridge. Like Rauma, it also has its own language. Aside from its Swedish influences, Närpiö is like other small towns and villages in Finland.

As in other places, the population is growing old gracefully. Some young people have already left, finding their way to larger cities such as Turku, Tampere or Helsinki for work, adventure or love. Some also attend university, and perhaps a few will return later when they inherit the responsibility of the family farm.

A small town square is bordered by shops and restaurants, although the hub has moved closer to the modern supermarket now. Close to this area is a bridge that arches over the river, gently flowing towards the sea.

Further down the river, some houses have long gardens ending at its bank. Most of these have a fishing stand or steps leading into the river. Many properties have a sauna, either close to the bank or further away, depending upon when and who had bought the building and obtained permission to construct it.

It wasn't the first time someone had fallen into the river. Alcohol can occasionally be a comfort to some people, especially in the darkness of wintertime. However, this time it was different. The river was completely frozen, and the sight which greeted an elderly lady walking over the bridge that morning, on her daily walk to collect fresh bread, was startling.

Henny Grövenpick had walked this way a thousand times. No, ten thousand times. She was actually wondering to herself that morning exactly how many times she had done so but couldn't begin to work it out.

Mrs Grövenpick hadn't owned a car since her husband Pasi died fifteen years ago, almost to the day. She didn't need to as she didn't live far from the town centre. Her morning walk, every morning, was possibly the main thing that kept her going these days. It was a reason to rise in the morning, helping to keep her healthy and active. The smell of fresh bread also brought the meaning of a new day back into the house. It reminded her of happier times when she and Pasi had enjoyed breakfast together for almost every day of their thirty-two years of marriage.

She was deep in thought that morning, and although slow in step, held her head higher than usual, as memories of her life flooded through her mind, as they often did. It was still quite dark, and Christmas lights twinkled around her, glistening on the purest, whitest snow. Her footsteps were the first to walk through the landscape that day. Large snowflakes were slowly falling and gently settling on and around her as she did so.

Mrs Grövenpick cast her eye over the side of the bridge as

usual and suddenly stopped. There was something on the ice. Something different. Something not quite right. She strained to see what it was; her eyesight was not as good as it used to be.

A tree, perhaps? Maybe an animal? Could something have fallen onto the ice?

She moved closer to the bridge. The dark blueness of the sky was beginning to give way to the first light of day, and she couldn't be entirely sure about what she was looking at.

Could it be a body? Could someone have drunk too much alcohol the night before and stumbled down to the icy river - to face fatal consequences?

Mrs Grövenpick wasn't sure what it was, but she was convinced that it wasn't right. She hastily shuffled off towards the town.

She walked to the small cafe, already open, with its lights twinkling and the strong smell of newly baked bread and cinnamon buns filling the air.

She uncharacteristically burst into the cafe and made her way to the counter while yelling out:

"I think someone has fallen onto the ice in the river!"

Everyone in the busy cafe froze. Just for a moment but a moment that seemed frozen in time while the assembled customers digested the news.

Someone from a table jumped up.

"Are you sure?"

"I think so."

The question had arisen from a man who'd been clearing the snow that morning; a large burly gentleman with a fluorescent jacket and conspicuous presence.

"Okay, let me take a look."

He dived out of the cafe while the remaining clientele burst into a chatter of questions, all relating to the elderly lady's comment.

"Come on now, dear," the owner, Pirjo, reassured her.

She took Mrs Grövenpick by the hand and sat her down. Then, she poured a cup of coffee into a mug on the table in front of her.

The burly man who'd left to check the situation appeared back in the doorway within a minute.

"She's right!" he said. "Call 112 (Finland's emergency number) now."

The café owner grabbed the phone but looked back helplessly at the man, waiting for some direction or words to be put into her mouth.

"That's alright; I'll do it."

He took the phone from her, putting his hand on her shoulder and dialling the national number for the emergency services.

The police station was nearby, and it didn't take long for a van to appear outside, its lights dancing in all directions from the glare of the snow.

An officer opened the cafe door, and after a brief exchange of words, the burly man went into the van with the policeman. They drove towards the bridge, with another police vehicle already drawing up by the cafe.

Officer Hannu Palmu was first at the scene, together with the burly man named Matti. They made their way down to the ice, pausing to survey the scene in front of them. It was growing lighter, and now clearly apparent what the object on the ice was:

a body lay motionless, and no cracks surrounded it.

The ice is probably a few centimetres thick already, thought Hannu.

Deciding to risk it, he edged his way closer, across the river. He could see a frozen circle of blood around the body, seemingly glueing it to the ice. Hannu shuddered for a moment as the cold mist of the morning rolled into the vista and began to chill him deep inside.

Hannu gingerly and carefully made his way next to the body. He knew from previous experience that the ice was thick enough to be walked upon. Still, he always made his way slowly and with an air of caution where a river was concerned. Lakes were straightforward, but rivers could be unpredictable. He had also seen dead bodies before but not quite like this one. The others had either been in car accidents or passed away in their sleep. This one was different.

The cause of death seemed obvious, with no attempt to disguise it. A hatchet was buried into the side of the man's head, which lay resting on the ice, with a vast pool of frozen blood encircling it. A towel was wrapped around the head as if an effort had been made to stop the bleeding. The corpse was long dead now and almost as white as its surroundings.

Up above, Hannu's colleagues had closed off the area, busy directing traffic across the bridge to minimise disruption to the day. Not that the traffic flow was necessarily heavy that morning, but there was enough movement towards the supermarket to necessitate control. Besides, not so much happened in Närpiö on a day-to-day basis. This situation could stop traffic for some time, especially with the amount of curiosity it would provoke.

By now, an ambulance and a fire engine had arrived. The police considered the necessity to lift the body out vertically, so the fire engine reversed into position. A police photographer also appeared, and a series of flashes broke through the morning mist.

Over the following few hours, the area around the river became a hive of activity, with the area containing the bridge being partially cordoned off by yellow tape, and blue lights coming and going.

It was a considerable effort to extract the body from the river. Following an exhaustive search for evidence around the immediate area, a sizeable part of the ice was removed to preserve any DNA. Finally, the body was cut from its icy grave and taken away to a more suitable resting place.

The investigation was quick to progress, and the man was identified as Pekka Kuusisto, a retired local farmer. Mr Kuusisto had been born, raised, schooled and then worked in Närpiö, hardly leaving the town during his whole life. He lived in the same house that his family had lived in for generations: a picturesque eggshell-blue building on the outskirts of the town, with a considerable swathe of land surrounding it. In the past, it had been farmed, but more recently, there'd been little point. Pekka had retired and the money to be earned from the land was not enough to make the effort worthwhile.

Over the years, as he had never married and had no offspring, he had sold land whenever he needed extra money, over and above his small income. He was not a rich man, nor was he poor. Comfortable would be the word to describe him. He was a regular at the supermarket and occasionally visited restaurants in town, preferring to eat out when he could afford to. He had sometimes been known to linger long at the cafe to catch up with the town's gossip, and like Mrs Grövenpick - he too had a penchant for fresh bread.

Pekka had been a collector, something to which he had dedicated his whole life. His house and the adjoining out-buildings were full of Finnish history regalia, together with a collection of American antiques and collectables. He had been particularly proud of a once-fine red Ford Mustang, which he had occasionally driven around town to considerable admiration. When not in use, it had been kept clean and shining in his barn, although it had degraded somewhat when he had decided not to drive anymore, a few years earlier.

When the police arrived at the victim's house, it was impossible to define the motive for his murder immediately. There was no evidence of a scuffle, and it was utterly impractical to decide if anything had been stolen. Theft could have been the motive, but there were so many collectables, there was no way of knowing if anything was missing. In addition, the police were puzzled why and how he got from the house to the river?

The investigation continued. An early discovery had been a missing painting. At least, there was the precise shape of a framed picture that may have been removed from the living room. This possibility was later verified by one of the neighbours who remembered seeing a painting there. He couldn't remember what building it was explicitly but recalled that Pekka had told him that the picture was of a street in Rauma.

There are little more than a hundred murders in Finland every year. For this reason, every police officer is aware of significant crimes like these, and they are published far and wide across the country.

Back in Rauma, an incident in Urjala was noted with more than a passing interest. Jussi had been scanning the police intranet for news before his routine patrol. It was with some excitement that he noted this new murder and the potential theft of a painting.

"I wonder if they're somehow connected?" he asked.

Jussi was talking to his partner, Harri, who was absentmindedly chewing a pen while relaxing in the cab of their police car. They were taking a break and both thinking of other things. Even though they got on well with each other, they found that small talk could be challenging and sometimes thinking took less effort.

"I have no idea," Harri replied. "It's a similar incident to the one in Urjala. But it's three hours away, and we don't know the motive for either incident, do we? However, you're right, there could be some connection. They weren't related by family, were they?"

"No, not from the brief I read, no visible connection so far anyway."

"Some maniac on the loose? Could be. You never know, and if it were a random homicide, it would be hard to track down."

"Well, let's hope they're neither related nor repeated; Harri, it's time to go home."

Jussi was keen to get home that evening. He had a trip to Helsinki waiting for him and was more excited than usual to finish his day. There would probably be an enjoyable and entertaining evening ahead of him, with his friend Heli. Police work was important, but it would also wait for a while.

When he arrived home, he immediately set about packing a bag. He had to leave the following day and would travel on Friday morning. He would stay in Helsinki until Sunday morning and make his way back in the afternoon; he had an early shift on Monday.

He had wondered whether to drive or catch a bus down. In the end, he favoured driving, as this put him in control of departing whenever he wanted. He didn't know how things would go with Heli and might decide to cut his weekend short if the situation became awkward. He didn't think it would do, but he didn't need any complications in his life.

He'd arranged to stay at the impressive Hotel Torni, downtown. It was a unique building due to its stature, position, architecture and design. He had stayed at the hotel before and liked it very much; it had real character and was well-placed for everything. It also benefited from a great bar on the top floor where he'd arranged to meet Heli for a pre-dinner drink. He could almost taste the mojito that he'd savoured several times in the bar. Although not a big drinker by any stretch, when off-duty he could certainly enjoy a glass of good red wine, ice-cold sauna beer or artfully-made mojito when the mood took him.

After neatly folding his clothes into a carry-on case, including his favourite shirt and jeans, he snapped it shut. Then he made a snack: a rye bread sandwich with cheese and ham, and washed it down with a cold light beer, as a start to his short break. Then, he turned in for the night, looking forward to the days ahead. He turned on the television and watched part of a reality music show before his eyelids became heavy.

Bzzzt! Bzzzt!

Jussi's phone shattered his slumber, and he instinctively grabbed at it, not yet having mentally clarified whether the sound was an alarm or a phone call.

It was a phone call. Jussi put it to his ear, noting with horror the time on his alarm clock, which stated in clear blue neon: 2.10 am.

"Argghhh, you've got to be kidding!" he muttered out loud. "Hello?"

"Jussi, it's Pekka. Look, I'm sorry to wake you, but there was a big RTA (road traffic accident) on the way to Pori, and most of the night team have been called to that."

"It's okay. What's up?" Jussi asked, managing to muster some enthusiasm.

"Well, it may be nothing, but we've had a report from someone just outside of town. The caller says that he's seen lights, maybe a torch, being used in a house where he thinks the owner is away."

"Okay, I'm on it. I'll use my own car and drive straight over."

Pekka gave him the address. Jussi threw on his uniform and was straight out of the apartment, into the car and gone within minutes. It wasn't usual for him to drive his car rather than going to the station first, but he didn't want to waste time getting a police vehicle. He just wanted to get back to bed.

As Jussi knew roughly the area in question, he was there within ten minutes flat.

A mixture of rain and wet snow was falling from the sky, resulting in a road covered with slush. Jussi turned into a small lane, actually a bumpy old track, and slowly made his way down it.

The way was dark, and he passed a couple of houses that, quite naturally at that time, were in complete darkness. It was impossible to tell which one was the exact address, but then he thought he spotted it.

As he approached, he switched his lights off, just in case. If there were to be an intruder, he wanted to catch them. This way, he would have the advantage of surprise. He was also aware that he should wait for backup if there was someone there.

The house looked dark and grim in the drizzling night. He parked the car in the yard by the barn and looked around. He hadn't seen anything on the way up the narrow driveway, and was scanning the area for anything unusual. After a minute of staring through the blackness, he took his torch from the glove compartment and opened the door.

After he got out of the car, he listened intently for another minute or so before he clicked on the powerful torch, and the shaft of light shone brightly across the barn. Jussi shone the light inside the barn entrance - it seemed to have been damaged in a fire at some point. He could see through one of the jagged openings, but wet wood was the only thing to discern. He continued to walk towards the barn, scanning his torch around the general area every few seconds.

Suddenly, light flooded the space from another source. Jussi instinctively held his hand over his eyes.

An engine roared to life somewhere, and the light quickly started to approach him. He was about to shout when he realised a vehicle was coming straight at him. He turned and ran. The engine was getting louder, and he could feel it getting closer and closer.

Jussi ran behind the barn and beyond; his torch flashing everywhere as he ran towards the field. Then he lost his balance and fell. As he did so, his head hit something hard, and he felt his consciousness fade as he dropped heavily to the ground.

◆ ◆ ◆

Jussi opened his eyes slowly, aware of a throbbing feeling inside his head and a pain on its right side. He could also taste blood in his mouth. He was cold and wet.

What happened?

He looked around. He could see a glint of light to his right-hand side as he dragged himself up to a sitting position. He crawled over and picked up the still-lit torch. He scanned it around and checked his surroundings to get his bearings. He suddenly remembered where he was: the farm, the barn.

How long have I been out? I need to get on my feet. Get up Jussi.

He struggled to stand up, but a combination of pain, weakness and the snow on the ground beat him back to his knees. He sat back and gave himself a moment. He didn't know how bad an injury he had sustained or if the reason he had fallen to the ground was still a threat.

Danger - his reflex made him turn off the torch and start moving towards a thicket of trees he could just make out about twenty metres away. He moved towards it by a mixture of walking and crawling and then grabbed a tree, spinning himself around the trunk and staring out into the dark, trying to see something through the blackness.

After a few minutes, the cold suddenly jarred him back into moving, and he slowly and painfully started to make his way over to, and then around, the barn. Staying low, he walked along the opposite side of the barn he had previously circumvented. He made his way forward, constantly monitoring for any new signs of danger. He waited there for a few minutes in silence.

Satisfied there was no longer a danger, he staggered to his car. He managed to get in, close the door, turn on the lights and engine, and lock the doors.

Just when he was planning his next move, the most welcoming sight of a blue flashing light appeared in his rear-view mirror from further down the track. It heralded the arrival of assistance. He opened the door and made his way towards it.

"What happened to you, Jussi?" A cheery voice asked him through the now-open car door.

Studying Jussi with both surprise and concern was Pekka.

"I tripped over something and banged my head. It hurts like hell," he grimaced, wiping blood off the side of his face. "Something dazzled me. There was a car here that suddenly switched its lights on and drove straight at me. Have you checked the house?"

"No, not yet. I wanted to check on you first. You know you should have waited for me, don't you?"

"Yeh, I know. I just wanted to check things out. There didn't seem to be anyone around at the time," Jussi replied.

While he was talking, Pekka made his way over to the police car and grabbed a first aid kit. His concern was growing about the blood trail down Jussi's face.

"Keep still. This isn't going to be pleasant."

Pekka wiped Jussi's head and placed a small field dressing over the top.

"It's not too bad - probably no hospital for you today unless you're feeling dizzy?"

"No, I'm fine", replied Jussi. "It's probably better than it looks, but not how it feels. Anyway, let's check the barn and then the house, shall we?"

The two officers searched the area, with torches illuminating every corner of the old barn. After briefly checking the small outbuildings, they walked to the house itself.

Everything seemed fine there; the house was secure. There were some tyre tracks on the ground, but with the continuously falling snow, the markings were already being filled.

It had been an average-sized car with newer studded winter tyres. Jussi deduced this from the tracks and called the station to give a brief report. He advised that there was no need for additional support yet, especially as the RTA situation was still drawing in resources from the whole area.

In the meantime, Pekka broke out some coffee from a flask in readiness to sit and wait. Even though the intruder had disappeared and the building secure, they felt obliged to remain and ensure that there was no repeat of the crime. In addition, they wanted to provide security for the neighbours, some of whom could already be seen a little way off, with their room lights on, wondering what the blue lights signalled?

After one hour, and one emptied coffee flask, they drove to the end of the track and remained there for a short time.

Harri looked at Jussi and piped up.

"Okay, Jussi. Get back to bed and rest. After dropping the van, I'll do the same and ask the lads to pop round during the night again. They can also talk to the neighbours in the morning."

Back at his apartment, Jussi surveyed his image in the mirror. Even after gently removing the excess blood, there wasn't any hiding the cut and bruise on the left side of his forehead. Luckily, it wasn't bleeding anymore, nor did it require stitches. However, he had lost his clean-cut image for his meet-up with Heli. He thought he looked more like a Friday night brawler than a policeman now.

Ah, what the hell, she will have to love it, he decided.

It was Friday morning, and Jussi started preparing for his date. He had the day off, so didn't need to hurry.

After a shower and shave, he had got a few things together and dropped them into his favourite overnight bag. The bag was well-used and was the handy type that you opened with a zip in a rectangle and everything just dropped in. It didn't take him long to fill it anyway, as he was a light traveller.

"Okay! I'm good to go!" he said out loud to his reflection.

He took one last look in the mirror, grimacing as he did so, opened the apartment door and carefully locked it behind him. He then strode purposefully over to his waiting car.

The temperature had improved a little, and he could already feel the change in the ground. The snow had started to melt into the earth, resulting in brown slush, leaching into the pure white of snow. He hoped this was not quite the end of the winter as it was much too early, and he never looked forward to the time of brown mush, ice and darkness. No, that period was better over in weeks rather than months, and later in the spring too.

Jussi took the main road in the direction of Turku, planning to drive until he hit the highway, then, after a couple of hours, straight to ring road number three. After that, it would be the airport. He guessed the journey would take around three hours, as the weather was fine, and he knew the route well.

I might also stop for a quick coffee on the way, he thought.

His head still throbbed from time to time, and he decided a short rest might be required at some point. He hadn't booked a hotel room, although he knew Heli had. They had been intimate before, and he expected they would spend the night together, more for friendship than anything else. However, if needed, Jussi had a backup plan to stay at an old police college friend's place.

The journey felt long and unpleasant. The weather had changed, and the wind and traffic whipped up the powdered snow like a whirlwind. Jussi didn't like this kind of weather and was now determined to make the whole journey all in one go.

No stops now, he thought to himself.

He gritted his teeth and drove into the snow flurries, made worse by the number of trucks on the road. Despite this, he pressed on and was able to reach Vantaa airport in good time.

He was pleased with himself when he reached the airport carpark, only slightly later than predicted. He promptly left and locked the car in a nearby multi-storey car park. Then he made a beeline for the cafe. He smiled as he ordered his drink with added flavour and foam. The designer coffee was a real treat as he didn't come here very often.

After a few minutes, he wandered over to view the bank of screens that displayed the flight arrival times, and began to check the list of flights. No sooner had he started doing this than who should come sweeping through the sliding door but Heli. He must have made some miscalculation in the timing as he wasn't expecting her for another hour.

Jussi moved quickly towards her, greeting her with affection. She looked good, actually terrific. Her blonde hair was neatly platted, and she wore a smart, fitted red coat over a tight white jumper, with black trousers and knee-length black boots. Angular, black plastic glasses framed her pretty, soft-featured face. She was wheeling a bright emerald green suitcase behind her.

"Wow, what happened - a strong tailwind?" asked Jussi.

"Not quite," Heli said. "They cancelled my flight, but as I only had hand luggage, they told me there was one leaving almost right away from another gate, if I ran. So that's what I did and I made it, and well, here I am!"

Heli beamed a smile, and Jussi wondered if the sparkle in her eyes was reflected in his own.

"That's great!" said Jussi.

"Oh, that looks good!" said Heli, spying his coffee and taking a sip. "Ugh, it's a bit too strong for me. I'd forgotten that about you. It's so great to see you," she exclaimed.

They made their way out of the terminal, with Heli's arm

linking with his. The weekend had started well.

ABOUT HELI

Five years earlier.

Heli sat on the steps of the old wooden pier, looking out across the lake at the opposite shore. The water was quite still this evening, with just an occasional little splash caused by a dragonfly or small fish breaking the surface. The air was warmer now, almost 24 degrees, and it felt like a balmy Mediterranean evening.

She sat on the steps so her toes could touch the water, moving them gently from side to side, causing small waves to ripple across the lake. She shook some of the water from her long, red, wet hair and smoothed it down over her head. She had been swimming that evening; in fact, it had been her third swimming session of the day. She loved being in the water in warm weather, and she loved the summer.

As she sat, she recalled memories of being with her mother when she was younger. She had been born in Helsinki, but her father had left before she was old enough to know him; he had since completely disappeared.

She remembered running along the beach and having fun with the sun shining. She would enjoy splashing around in the water and swimming, 'like a fish,' as her mother used to say. The memory was from more than fifteen years ago, but she remembered it as if it happened yesterday. Unfortunately, her mother had died two years ago. Today, she remembered some of their happier memories, which always made her smile.

Alone with her thoughts, Heli's mind wandered. She imagined herself walking across a sandy beach, with the waves lapping at her feet as the tide came in. The sun was on her back, and she was making her way to a cabin across the soft sand.

Heli loved travelling and, despite the country's attractions, in her heart of hearts, was not sure if she would see out the rest of her life in Finland. Her experiences had made her stronger and more independent. She wanted to see the world and experience it to the full.

"What are you thinking about?" asked a voice behind her, breaking her train of thought.

She looked around and saw Jussi standing behind her, with a drink in each hand.

"Nothing special, just hoping for more warm days ahead."

Jussi approached, and she shuffled along the pier to make room for him to sit beside her.

"Thank you," she said, gratefully accepting the ice-cold drink. "By the way, what is this?" she asked with a suspicious smile.

"This, Heli, is a mojito!"

"Oh, Wow! I've never had a homemade one. Of course, I've drunk a few of those amazing ones at the Torni Bar over the years, but you made this? Now, I'm impressed!"

She sipped the drink and tasted the sharp citrus freshness combined with mint, powerful rum, and the sweetness of sugar.

"Oh yes, this is perfect. Where did you learn to make this?" Heli asked.

"That would have to be a secret between a bartender and me," he winked.

"Well, please say a thank you from me next time you see him."

"Err - it was a 'she' actually, but don't worry, our relationship was strictly based on mojitos."

Heli laughed and gave him a light dig in the ribs with her elbow.

It'd been a perfect day. The sun had been shining all day long, and the temperature had hit the dizzy heights of thirty degrees at one point, very warm for Finland.

They had rented a log cabin for the weekend near Lohja, about forty minutes from Helsinki. The cabin owner had a couple of kayaks available, so Jussi had rented them both. They had spent the morning kayaking around the islands and swimming in the lake.

At lunchtime, they had eaten sausages, grilled on the barbeque by Jussi, and a fresh salad with lettuce, melon, tomatoes, avocados and cashew nuts, prepared by Heli. Afterwhich they had relaxed and then gone swimming again.

Jussi had enjoyed their kayaking adventure. Except for a couple of trips, he hadn't spent long in a kayak before and resolved to go more often in future.

"I'm hungry again!" exclaimed Heli.

"Me too!" agreed Jussi.

"Are you ready for the best-grilled steak you've ever tasted?"

"And are you ready for the biggest salad you have ever seen?" Heli responded.

They both agreed with each other, stood up and walked along the wooden pier towards the shore. The pier continued onto the beach, where the owner had made a small sandy area, where they left the kayaks. Heli took Jussi's hand and stepped off the pier, walking through the sand in her bare feet. She loved having her toes in the sand and smiled at Jussi as she did so. He knew she would do this, as she had done it a few times already that day. He was happy to oblige her.

They were dressed in t-shirts and shorts due to the evening's warmth, but as they walked through the trees, Heli suddenly slapped her leg.

"Ah, mosquito bite!" she exclaimed. "Let's jog through these trees, come on!"

So, they jogged up the path to the cabin and onto the terrace. The cabin was in a large clearing that helped avoid the insects that were now descending from the trees en masse.

They spent the next hour preparing food and arranging a romantic dining area. Heli placed a red-checked table cloth onto the heavy wooden table. Jussi lit some small candles and put them on the table and around the terrace. He uncorked a bottle of red wine, his favourite: Malbec from Argentina, and then finished the steaks on the barbeque.

They were more than ready for food when they sat down to eat. They both thoroughly enjoyed their meal.

Jussi regarded Heli for a few moments and recalled when he had first met her.

It had been Pitsiviikko (Lace Week) in Rauma. Heli had been visiting the city for the first time. As Jussi wandered around the market stalls, he couldn't help noticing her. She had long red hair, a white polo shirt, and small, black lace shorts. He strolled over to the stall where she was examining some leather bracelets.

"I would choose that one," Jussi suggested to the girl.

She looked up and smiled at him, "Why? I can't decide between them."

"I think the red in this one goes with your hair," he said.

The girl laughed, "I'm not sure whether that's a recommendation or a chat-up line. Which is it?"

"Okay, busted. I just thought I would come over and say hello."

She turned around a little further and said,"Well, Hello. My name is Heli, and you are...?"

"Jussi."

"Well, Jussi, it's nice to meet you. Do you know what?"

"What?"

"I'm going to take the red one," and with that, she paid the stall-holder and put the bracelet on.

"Could you help me with the clasp?" she asked

"Of course."

Jussi closed the lock, holding her wrist as he did so.

"Thanks for your advice, Jussi. Hey, I'm thirsty. Should we grab a drink?"

And from that point, they quickly became what some might describe as an item. Jussi had been on vacation from the police college in Tampere, and Heli had been on a four-week break from her job at an art gallery in Helsinki. Neither had any particular commitments, so they spent time in Eura, where Jussi lived, and then in Helsinki, where Heli lived. Now they were at a cabin they had rented for a long weekend.

Jussi hadn't really had a serious girlfriend before, although he had experienced several short relationships. The feeling he had now was new to him, and he was enjoying it.

Heli had recently completed her Master's Degree in Art History. Now, with her first real job, she was a single girl with money and was enjoying her life in Helsinki. She was becoming very fond of Jussi, though. After these fantastic three weeks, she had started to wonder what might happen at the end of their holiday. She broached the subject that evening.

"So, our holiday comes to an end next week. I've enjoyed the time we've spent together, Jussi. It's a shame we live so far away from each other."

"Yeh, I've been thinking the same. I still have more studies in Tampere, and then I'll start my first job with the police. Time goes quickly, though."

"It does. I really enjoy my job in Helsinki, Jussi. Also, the gallery is part of a large organisation, so it has opportunities in other countries, so I'm hoping I'll get some international experience, one day. Maybe you will visit me?"

They chatted for some time about the subject. It seemed that although they had enjoyed their time together and were getting closer every day, their careers would take them in different directions.

After a while, they dropped the subject and returned to just enjoying each other's company. Later, they moved to the bedroom and let their feelings take over.

The weekend passed quickly, too quickly for both of them. They packed up the cottage on the final day and waved goodbye to it. They each secretly hoped they would visit it again together someday.

When it was time to leave, Jussi took Heli home in his car. It wasn't the most talkative journey as they both had things on their mind.

At her apartment building, they held each other for a while. Neither wanted to make their goodbye more difficult than it was. Afterwards, Jussi drove back to Eura with mixed feelings. Then, he received a phone call.

"Jussi, Moi. It's me."

"I guessed it was. Missing me already?" Jussi smiled.

"Of course. Hey, I have some news. I've just received an email and found out I have an offer to transfer to London. Isn't that amazing?"

"That's great Heli. You'll have a fantastic time. Will you take the job?"

At that moment, their minds briefly considered other possibilities.

Then, "Yes. I will. I may never get this opportunity again."

"I'm so happy for you Heli. When will you leave?" Jussi asked.

"Soon, I think. Someone has just left and they need a replacement quickly."

With that, they completed their call, wished each other well, and hoped they would meet or talk again soon.

They both had strong feelings for each other but it was clear that the road would soon take them in different directions. It would be some time before circumstances would bring them together once again.

THE REUNION

The Present Day.

After collecting Heli from the airport, Jussi drove to downtown Helsinki. He found a tight parking space around the corner from the hotel and unloaded their bags. They walked up the hotel steps, and as they did so, Heli linked her arm with his once again. It happened quite naturally, just as she used to do. As they walked towards the entrance, Jussi coughed and made his admission, his voice faltering nervously.

"Heli, I just want to check something."

She looked at him expectantly.

"Well, I wasn't sure about his, but I didn't book a separate room. We could ask for one with twin beds, though?"

Heli laughed and looked coyly at him.

"Well, I'm sure that you can book one now, can't you?"

Jussi's face flushed red with embarrassment.

"Don't worry, I booked a double room," she added with a cheeky grin.

A smile crossed Jussi's face, and he gave her a friendly dig in the ribs, at which they both laughed.

After checking in, they made their way up to the room using the tiny, old, creaking lift. As they did, Heli leaned over, and they kissed; it was a slow lift.

The room was impressively designed, with tall windows, and as Jussi noted, a comfortable bed. They dropped their bags and quickly got ready to leave. The view from the window was in the direction of the city, and Jussi took it in for a moment while Heli freshened up after her journey.

Jussi walked down to the reception area, using the stairs for exercise and also to look around the hotel. At the same time, Heli made a short phone call that she explained was necessary for work. She reappeared after about twenty minutes.

It was snowing much harder outside now. As the couple walked out of the hotel, they began to run, the kind of running people do when they don't want to fall over on a slippery surface but want to get somewhere fast.

Jussi had booked a special restaurant. It was one they had dined at, before they had gone their separate ways. They arrived at the restaurant within minutes and were welcomed inside by a smiling waiter and the warmth of a roaring fire. They quickly ordered a couple of glasses of warming glögi: hot berry juice with the traditional addition of raisins, almonds and on this occasion, Finnish vodka. The drink was perfect for that moment.

The evening felt as if they had never parted. The couple talked rapidly, frequently remembering their collective histories. Each one of them was fascinated by the newer stories of the other. When reminding each other of their older stories, they even finished off one another's sentences.

Their conversation was interrupted from time to time with delicious food, as the menu stated, all sourced locally. They ate wild mushrooms, organic vegetables and fresh perch spiked with dill. Everything was washed down with a deliciously crispy, ice-cold white wine.

While they were talking and waiting for their desserts, the subject of the paintings came up.

"So, what are you working on at the moment, Jussi? Anything exciting?" she asked eagerly.

"Well, the usual selection of traffic offences and drinking issues. No doubt at this rate I will make detective in no time at all," Jussi laughed.

Heli returned his smile. She was very proud of Jussi and loved the fact that he was a policeman and doing well in his career. However, she did wonder how he could survive in a small town, with his level of drive and previously-held ambitions.

"Well, actually, there is something else that is quite interesting. It seems that I may be the only one who sees the big picture of the case, but I have to say, it's still a little blurry for me too."

"Can you tell me more?" Heli asked eagerly.

Happy to have found a confidant, Jussi told the whole story, at least as much as he thought he could.

The desserts arrived. They were presented with delicious plates of cloudberries and blueberries with warm vanilla sauce. These dishes were eaten rapidly with a tiny expresso; tea for Heli. Following this, cognacs were subsequently ordered and brought to the table.

"Wow, I can't believe all of that has happened in sleepy Satakunta!"

Heli's mouth was agape as she took another small sip of the strong warming liquid.

"Well, what do you think? Is there a connection between everything?" asked Jussi.

Heli thought for a moment.

"It does seem rather coincidental that all of these events concern paintings, and by the sound of it possibly by the same artist. But why? I've never heard of that artist, and from what you describe, they're nice paintings but nothing that special or unusual. Why would someone go to such lengths and possibly kill to get their hands on them?"

"Well, you never know with criminals, there are some very dangerous ones around, with dangerous minds. It could also be some a maniac with a fixation for something, that's if there is any link at all."

"We have some time tomorrow. Why don't we drop by the library and do some research?" suggested Heli excitedly.

"Well, that's not exactly how I had planned our weekend together," Jussi replied, laughing.

"Nonsense. It sounds like great fun. Why don't we go to the library after breakfast, then somewhere nice for lunch and go on from there to see some sights? I would also love to catch that new exhibition in Kiasma if we can."

"That sounds like a great plan," agreed Jussi, and he drained his glass.

The snow had stopped outside and the cold, crisp night was beckoning them, with twinkling lights from the trees above.

They walked back to the hotel almost as quickly as they had done to the restaurant. This time, it was for a different reason. Jussi had planned mojitos at the bar on the top floor of the hotel but they didn't make it that far. The room offered a much warmer atmosphere, and with their clothes quickly strewn around the floor, they soon melted into bed together, enjoying their mutual warmth.

All too soon, it was morning. Sunlight streamed through the tiny slits in the curtains. Jussi stirred and stretched, slowly opening his eyes. It had been the best Friday night for a long time.

He glanced over and noted Heli was still completely asleep with her hand hanging over her head. Jussi smiled at this familiar sleeping position and crept out of bed. He had arranged breakfast by quietly hanging out the card on the door in the early hours.

He quickly made himself look decent again in time for the arrival of a huge silver breakfast tray which appeared at the door, brought by a smiling waiter. Jussi received it and took the tray over to the bed. Hearing the clinking of breakfast, Heli awoke with a smile.

"Good morning!" he said.

"Good morning you," Heli replied sleepily and returned his smile.

Jussi poured tea and coffee, and they sat together in bed, diving hungrily into the breakfast of muesli, scrambled eggs and freshly-made pastries.

After a long and relaxing breakfast, they showered, dressed and left the hotel.

The day was cold and sunny. What a change it was from the day before. It was a lovely winter's morning, with icicles sparkling in the sun, high up on the rooftops of the old buildings.

They arrived at the brand-new library, named Oodi: an impressive and modern glass structure that looked even more magnificent than usual in that light.

The library had just opened its doors that morning and was still almost empty. They passed a few tourists, and there were a couple of other people browsing nearby. They went straight to the arts section and spent some time combing through some of the bookshelves for a book that might mention the artist in question. It was a fruitless exercise, though.

After a while, Heli had an idea. They made their way to the information desk to ask about the directory of books or any other way to locate some information on the artist.

"Yes, I can certainly help with that," the librarian answered.

She directed them towards a bank of computers at the back, and explained how they could search for items of interest from the files.

After only a short while engaged in this, Heli exclaimed, "Hey, I've found something!"

Jussi shunted over on his chair with wheels, and they examined her find. It was an old newspaper article from Laitila, which featured one of the artist's paintings and a photograph of him in his studio. They settled down to read it.

Stefan Hämäläinen was a Finnish artist, with Russian roots from his mother's side of the family. There was a description of the history of his artistic career. The newspaper article seemed to be a local hero piece, where a personality was selected to be featured. The report provided some of the information Jussi had already found during his internet search. Still, there were a couple of other interesting details.

Firstly, Stefan started his painting career relatively late in life but had been very prolific in his work. The article mentioned that he had painted a series of paintings portraying Rauma. These were to be exhibited in various places around Finland: a mix of larger cities and smaller locations. The collection consisted of six paintings in all.

Heli was very interested in art, not just because of her job but also because she had completed an art history degree at university. She studied the featured painting with more than a passing interest. She commented that it was nice but not spectacular, nor inspirational.

They completed their reading session, having found this was the only reference to Stefan, except for an article relating to the artist's death and a summary of the investigation. There were no heirs or surviving relatives available either. So that was that.

After their morning of research, they decided it was time for a break and a much-needed warming drink. The library was impressive but hadn't been the cosiest of places to spend the morning hours. They found a small cafe nearby, with just a few tables inside, and ordered mugs of hot chocolate.

"So, what do you think? asked Jussi. "Can you see something in that painting worth a million euros? Or do you think the artist stole someone's idea for a painting and was killed by a jealous psychopath?"

Heli chuckled, despite the serious undertones of the subject.

"I really don't know, Jussi."

He had been thinking all morning about it, and although he still believed there was some kind of connection between the events, he couldn't connect the dots.

After their drinks, they adjourned to the Kiasma art gallery. They had decided they would go there next and follow it with a long lunch.

On arrival, Jussi walked with Heli, deep in thought, as she waxed lyrical about the various works on display. He didn't share her passion for art, except for photography. However, he enjoyed it casually, and the time passed pleasantly enough, especially as he benefited from Heli's detailed knowledge of the subject. Throughout their gallery tour, though, his mind kept wandering back to the morning's research and the strange events in and around Rauma.

"I have an idea!" he exclaimed suddenly.

Heli eyed him with bemusement, especially as she was about to launch into a comprehensive explanation of the dramatic painting in front of them, featuring an old ship on a stormy night.

"Let's find the journalist who reported that article. They will probably be the only one that could give us more useful information."

"Good idea," said Heli. "Okay, I'll make you a deal. Let's finish here and then we can go and get the journalist's name from the library. Then you owe me the best salmon soup I have ever had."

Jussi smiled. Salmon soup had always been her favourite, and he could imagine how much she would have been missing it while away from Finland.

And that is how they found themselves in a small cosy restaurant with unremarkable style but with delicious salmon soup, washed down perfectly with ice-cold beers in frosted glasses.

After lunch, Jussi checked the internet on his mobile phone for the journalist's details. It seemed that Emma Korhonen had worked for the local newspaper for fifteen years and was now retired, living in Laitila, not too far from Rauma. No contact details were available, but he logged into the police database to search for them. There was an address but nothing more.

That's a matter for later, he decided.

Right now, they had a more pressing engagement and headed back to the hotel hand-in-hand.

"Thanks for your help Heli. I've decided to visit our reporter lady next week when I return to Rauma. It's a shame you can't be there! We make a great team!"

"Well, actually, now you bring it up, I have a small surprise for you. Things have changed at work recently, and as it turns out, I'll be able to stay in Finland for another week at least. So, I would be more than happy to spend some time in Rauma and give you a hand with some more research, among other things." she said with a wink, adding, "Unofficially, of course."

Jussi's face lit up. He couldn't have been more delighted and certainly didn't have to think about the suggestion for long.

"It's a deal! Let's drive up tomorrow afternoon, stay at my place, and I can show you around Rauma again. Although I have to work, I'm sure I can move some overtime hours around to get more free time together. Do you have to work as well?"

"Yes, but I can do most of it by computer and phone, so we should have plenty of time together."

At this, they both smiled.

The next day started late, after another pleasantly delicious lie-in.

After breakfast, the couple made their way into the shopping district. They whiled away some time, doing Christmas shopping in the big department stores around Aleksanterinkatu (Alexander Street). Next, they scouted in the small niche boutiques just out of the centre, down the side roads.

After a busy morning, it was time for lunch. Given Jussi and Heli's appetites over the past few days, they chose a lighter option. Entering a big department store, they took the lift to the top floor and ordered salads, which were served almost immediately.

During deliciously fresh Asian chicken salads, they were suddenly interrupted by a call on Heli's mobile.

"Hello," answered Heli.

Over the following minutes, there followed a succession of affirmations: yes, okay, understood, right and very well. Jussi tuned out for a moment, assuming the call didn't involve him and made his way to the bathroom.

He returned after a few minutes, just as Heli was ending her conversation. She turned towards him.

"I'm sorry, Jussi, but that was my Boss from London. He has an urgent matter that he wants me to deal with. Someone from Helsinki wants to invest a considerable amount of money in one of our new projects and discuss it further. Hence, as I am in Helsinki, he asked me to meet with her."

"Oh, that's a coincidence and also a shame! I mean, I'm sure it's a good opportunity for you and your company, but it's disappointing that you can't come with me to Rauma."

Jussi's face must have fully expressed his feelings as Heli quickly replied.

"Oh no, it's fine. I can still come to Rauma! It's just that I have to meet them tomorrow in the city. Why don't you do your interview with the lady in Laitila while I'm busy here? Then I can catch a bus to Rauma, and you can collect me from the bus station when I arrive. I'm sorry Jussi, does this sound okay?"

A grin came over Jussi's face, and he nodded with enthusiasm. They finished lunch and made for the hotel, where Heli made arrangements at reception to stay another night as Jussi packed his bag and prepared to leave.

The light was already dimming as he said goodbye to Heli. It was much nicer to drive at least part of the way in the light, so he quickly pulled on his gloves, walked around to the car and set off on his trip back to Rauma.

It felt like a long journey this time, but Jussi was happy his weekend had been so enjoyable. Now, he was now looking forward to returning home. He liked to travel occasionally but enjoyed his own place, with everything just as he wanted it. With Heli coming, it would make a pleasant change to have some company for a while.

Jussi stopped for a coffee, with a rye bread and cheese sandwich, at one of the service stations near the entrance to Lohja, some fifty kilometres from Helsinki. It was starting to get cold. He noted the temperature was dropping to minus fourteen degrees on the dashboard thermometer.

Time to get back home.

He didn't stop again until he arrived in the yard of his apartment.

The remainder of his evening was spent watching an action movie he had been saving for just such an occasion - when he would feel like doing nothing in particular. He sank further and further into the sofa, and relaxation eventually turned into sleep in his warm living room.

Outside, the temperature continued to drop. The weather forecast had said the temperature would drop even more, to as much as minus twenty-two degrees that night.

MORE REVELATIONS

The following day, Jussi arose bright and early. He had to work that morning, not an early shift this time, but the morning and the first part of the afternoon. His day was to be spent at the office, completing some pressing paperwork concerning recent events. He diligently finished it on his computer and then, later that morning, did some research on the journalist in Laitila.

During this time, he discovered the journalist's telephone number. He decided to speculatively call her and ask if he could arrange a time to discuss the paintings. It was a good decision, as the lady was delighted to have the opportunity to discuss the pictures and their history. There seemed no doubt that the prospect of receiving a new visitor with whom to talk was also a source of some considerable excitement for her.

After finishing work, Jussi walked home quickly. He changed into thick, layered casual clothing for the still-freezing weather and drove the forty minutes to Laitila.

After meandering around some houses on the outskirts of town, he eventually found the road and the house number he was searching for.

It was a traditional, old wooden house, set some way back from the road. It had a long pathway leading up to it, protected by a prickly and somewhat overgrown hedge.

Jussi opened the gate and trudged up the snowy path, which looked as if it had not been cleared for days. A light in the hallway encouraged him to press the button to ring the bell. He heard some activity from inside, and after a couple of minutes, saw someone through the glass panel, reaching to open the door.

"Hello, who's there?" a shrill voice asked, as a lady partially opened the door.

"Hello Ms Korhonen. It's Jussi, from the police. We spoke on the telephone earlier today."

"Oh yes, do come in," the lady replied in a welcoming tone.

The door opened and an elderly lady, smelling of lavender, beckoned Jussi into the narrow hallway. He brushed his feet on the mat, removed his shoes and placed his coat on one of the wooden pegs by the doorway.

"Thank you for seeing me today, Mrs Korhonen." offered Jussi.

"Tervetuloa (Welcome). Thank you for coming, young man. I don't receive many visitors these days. If I can talk about art, my favourite subject, it makes me even happier. Oh, and please call me Emma, unless you have come here to sell me something."

She laughed and went to the kitchen to arrange refreshments.

As she prepared the coffee, together with some warm pulla, Jussi made himself comfortable on the small sofa. He gratefully accepted a cup and explained his interest in the paintings, specifically the artist in question: Stefan Hämäläinen.

"I remember Stefan very well," she began in a quiet voice. "He had Russian parents if I remember correctly. I think some of his family were originally from Saint Petersburg."

She pulled a thick woollen shawl further around her shoulders as Jussi leaned in closer to hear.

"He was a very prolific painter. Some of the paintings were good; some were not so good. What was impressive was the sheer number of pieces he produced within his life - so many of them. He was somewhat of a recluse and lived way out in the countryside, with little interest in meeting people. He was nice enough, though, and usually attended the events where his work was exhibited, especially in Rauma and Laitila. You had to get to know him, and it took a while to do that. I do remember some very nice conversations with him about..."

Her voice trailed off into the distance as if remembering one of them.

"Did you know he had died?" Jussi interjected.

He didn't want to offer any of the circumstances in case it would upset the old lady.

"Oh yes, that was a bad business. I read about it in the local newspaper."

Jussi was relieved not to have to break this news and nodded his head.

"Did you hear that some of his paintings may have gone missing or been damaged?"

He waited for a minute as Emma searched her memory once more, then she finally shook her head. Jussi spotted a golden opportunity to discover more information and perhaps solidify his chain of thought on recent events.

"Do you happen to know if he painted any pictures of Rauma?" he asked.

"Oh yes! Of course, he did."

Jussi's eyes widened, and he prompted her to continue.

“He painted, 'The Paintings of Rauma,' you know," which she said as if it were something that everyone would know.

He beckoned her to continue.

"Well, The Paintings of Rauma were a series of paintings commissioned by the city of Rauma to celebrate their anniversary. I forget which one. Anyway, he painted six beautiful paintings of the old town. Yes, it was six. They were of different views, such as the old houses, the town square and the church - things like that."

"Ahhh. Were the pictures particularly good? Did they become well-known? Or valuable?" Jussi asked earnestly.

"Well, they were rather good, and they received a lot of press at the time because they were of the city. Particularly, people in Rauma talked about them, of course. I know they were exhibited in the local museum for some time, but I think some were sold later to raise money after people lost interest. They did keep some, though, I think. I remember one, or maybe two, went to the Municipal Museum Association in Helsinki. Oh yes, he kept one of them. I remember him telling me specifically. it was his favourite view of Rauma, you see."

She drifted off once more as if deep in thought.

"Mrs Korhonen, I mean Emma, do you know why anyone might kill someone to own one or more of these paintings?"

"Good gracious, no dear. The pictures were good but not that good. Unless you were from Rauma, you probably wouldn't be interested in them at all. Well, perhaps as a tourist maybe? But to kill for them, no, no, no," she replied, shaking her head.

They talked more about the story, and the paintings as Jussi munched his way through a second pulla and drank hot black coffee.

After an hour and a half, he had finished, and the conversation had run its course. Jussi made ready to leave and thanked Emma for her help. He also left his email address and telephone number should anything else of interest occur to her. He had enjoyed the conversation and was happy to bring some life into Emma Korhonen's house that day. She had also clearly enjoyed his visit and talking about her memories.

Before he left, he asked for something to clear the snow and spent twenty minutes completing the task outside. Emma was delighted.

When Jussi returned to the car, he searched for Heli's phone number and pressed the call button. The phone rang out several times, but there was no answer.

Oh well, Jussi thought to himself. *She will call me when she is on her way.*

With that, he started the engine and drove off into the night towards Rauma.

The sky was clear now, and the temperature dropping, but Jussi was pleased to see the stars and the pure whiteness of the road: winter in Finland had its compensations.

Things were beginning to come together in his mind. With the 'Paintings of Rauma' revelation, he was convinced about a connection between the Rauma museum break-in, the stolen paintings, the murder of the farmer in Urjala, the murder of the artist and possible theft of one or more pictures in Närpiö.

Who knows? Perhaps more of the paintings have been stolen elsewhere? he asked himself.

Whatever the answer, it seemed that 'The Paintings of Rauma' somehow connected them all. But why? Six rather good paintings, of which a few may now have gone missing, without any particular value.

On his way back to Rauma, driving through snow, these thoughts circulated around and around in Jussi's head. He couldn't think of any motive for murder.

When he arrived home, something more pressing began to trouble him. He hadn't heard anything from Heli, and there was no answer from her mobile phone either. He tried multiple times again, and the call just rang out. There was also no message facility enabled, which was odd. Perhaps it was the way his mind was working at the moment regarding recent events. He began to get concerned.

No, it's nothing, he told himself. *Heli is delayed in her meeting, and the best thing that I can do now is to prepare the house for her arrival.*

He was thinking of tidying up, cleaning the bathroom, buying some flowers and good wine and lighting a couple of candles. This way, he could impress her with his home. He surveyed the room.

Hmmm. There's alot to do. Time to get on with it.

By 8 pm, the apartment was ready. There was still no news of Heli, though. He had put her lateness down to a car breakdown or bad weather and hoped to hear from her soon, or else hear a knock at the front door at any moment.

Then, his mobile phone suddenly rang out, and he smiled as he answered. It was the call he had been expecting, with Heli's name registering on the screen.

"Hi, where have you been?" Jussi asked cheerfully.

"Be quiet, please. Listen carefully," a voice answered.

Jussi was taken aback for a moment as it was undoubtedly not Heli's voice. Instead, it was that of a male: deep and with a slight accent. He couldn't place its owner, and searched for the reason why it wasn't Heli's voice.

"Who is this?" he demanded.

"Never mind that. We have your woman, and we need to meet with you tonight."

Jussi's heart was racing, although his professional police training had already kicked in.

"What woman are you talking about? And who are you?"

"We have your woman. Her name is Heli. You will come to this address in two hours."

The voice was rough and threatening. Jussi was trembling a little as it stated the address, which appeared to be in the middle of nowhere.

"If you so much as touch Heli, you'll be sorry," Jussi stated clearly.

"Calm down, she is fine, and no harm will come to her, provided you come here tonight, and we can talk. However, you must come alone, or things will go very bad for her."

Jussi didn't have to ask what he meant by that, as none of his thoughts worked out well for Heli.

"Alright, I will come there alone, and I expect to leave with Heli; do you know I'm a police officer?" he asked incredulously.

"Yes, we know everything about you, and now we need to have some information from you. This is just a simple exchange. Please don't be late."

The phone fell silent. Jussi glanced at his watch and noted he was due at the given address at 10 pm. It was now 8.05 pm. He quickly punched the address into his GPS and saw that it would take about one hour to get there. The meeting place was north-east of Rauma, towards the city of Pori and then towards the east, by a large lake named Isojärvi.

He considered his plan, of which the core objective was to get Heli out in one piece. If possible, his other goal was to arrest the person or persons who seemed to have kidnapped her. It didn't take long for him to decide that he would get there as quick as possible, park some distance away and work his way around the lake until he could find out what was going on. Then, he could decide to jump them by surprise or choose another approach.

His training as a police officer had taught him that the more information he had about a situation, the better. He thought of calling his closest colleagues in the police; however, he dismissed this thought quickly as he had no wish to put Heli in any danger.

What possible information could these people want from me anyway? Jussi asked himself.

He put on extra layers of thermal clothing. No doubt it would be freezing in the forest, and he would probably be outside for some time. He completed his outfit with a warm hat, a powerful torch and his service weapon. He had never discharged his firearm in the field, and he quickly checked it to ensure all was well and fully loaded. He felt comforted by it, although he sincerely hoped he wouldn't have to use it for the first time that night.

After his preparation, he jumped into the car and left, his tyres spinning in the snow as he accelerated out of his yard onto the open road. Jussi had only one thing on his mind at that moment.

I must get Heli back.

THE COTTAGE

Jussi stopped the car and studied his GPS closely. He decided this must be the place. He switched off his lights and pulled into the narrow road, after which he turned off the ignition and got out of the car. He decided to work his way around the side of the lake until he got to the cottage and see what he could discover without making himself known.

He still had around forty-five minutes left before the appointed time and estimated that it wouldn't take much more than ten minutes to reach the meeting point. He placed his pistol and torch into his coat pocket and started to move into the forest.

It was dead silent, save for the occasional sound of a duck hopping across the ice and an owl's distant hoot from across the lake. Where it wasn't iced over, the water was perfectly still, like a pool of glistening oil, with occasional concentric rings caused by a fish or a bird.

Jussi slowly crept through the trees surrounding the lake towards the cottage. He was aware that against the deathly silent backdrop, his steps seemed to amplify in volume - crunching loudly in the night. He stopped every few metres to check the surroundings and listen for other sounds, lest he might be discovered.

He knew the cottage must be close by, but this was a big lake. Although not immediately apparent, every seventy to one hundred metres, there was a cottage, outhouse, wood store or sauna building visible through the trees.

At this time of year, most of the cottages were closed and locked up, having been prepared for winter. Now they were waiting dormant until the ice changed into melting drops of water over the porches, heralding the first advent of spring.

How will I know which cottage it is? he thought, his eyes straining through the darkness.

Jussi hoped to glimpse a light somewhere, or the orange glow of a fire or even a television, to signal his destination. He checked his phone was still readily available and clipped to his side. He only intended to use it to call for backup if needed but was very aware that if he did need help, it would take time to arrive. Still, it comforted him on that freezing night as he carefully continued on his way.

Suddenly he froze.

He had spotted something directly ahead, lit by the moon. A shadow had moved on a distant terrace of a log cottage close by the lake. He dropped to his knees, aware of a slight cracking noise underfoot as he did so; the shadow didn't seem to move, though. Jussi held his breath.

After a short while, he allowed tiny breaths to escape through his nose. His hand rested on his gun, but he didn't want to unclip it for fear of making a noise and being discovered. Anyway, there was still a good chance that it wasn't the correct place. So, he waited.

It seemed like an age that he froze there. He began to feel an uncomfortable chill, slowly penetrating his layers of clothing.

Now, he was squinting ahead.

Is that a person over there?

As time passed, he started to feel that the shape was perhaps a tree, a shadow or even his imagination. Then, suddenly he saw a small light and the subsequent orange glow of a cigarette being smoked.

Yes, it is someone. The question is - Who? And is it one of them?

Jussi gradually sank further down, placing his hands onto the ground and lowering himself to a commando's crawling position. This reminded him of his national service in the Finnish army, which had been spent training for some future eventuality. Now, he was glad of the skills he had learned there.

When he was almost lying down, he slowly crawled forward, flinching at every crack of a twig or break of ice. As he moved forward, he didn't take his eyes off the figure on the cabin terrace.

A couple of times, he made a noise and thought he saw the figure look towards him but decided that he was far enough away for the sound not to have been heard. Besides, many indiscernible noises came from a forest on a winter's night. If someone heard something, it would probably just be taken for an animal, perhaps a fox or deer.

After what seemed like an age, the figure turned sharply around. Then, it walked to the cabin, opened a door and went inside.

As Jussi heard the door close, he breathed a long sigh of relief and checked his watch. He had around twenty-five minutes left until the deadline. He moved forward and then slowly to the side of the cabin wall, raising himself to his full height and flattening himself against it. He slowly edged his way along the wall until he reached the start of the terrace.

The windows were still too high, and he couldn't see anything on the terrace, so he crept silently over the terrace's log-fence and once again slid down to a low position, on all fours. Next, he hugged the wall next to the window as he raised himself again. He peered in, just at the edge, to view the scene inside.

He didn't have much time, and it would have to be soon if he were going to act.

Inside, the room was dim, with a small light in a corner and a roaring fire dancing in the fireplace. There was just enough light to discern the interior. Illuminated by a light in the corner, were two men talking to each other. He also noted a seated figure, watching television in the far corner of the room.

Jussi took a sharp intake of breath as the figure moved, and he saw it was Heli, sat in a rocking chair. He thought that she must be restrained in some way but didn't know for sure.

He withdrew from the window and tried to collect his thoughts and make a plan. He must have been concentrating too hard as he didn't notice any approach behind him nor hear any noise that would have made him turn around.

The next thing he heard was a click near his right ear and a soft-accented female voice.

"Alright, Mr Policeman, let's go inside," the voice whispered seductively.

Jussi turned his head slightly and saw the barrel of a gun through the corner of his left eye and a dark shape behind it.

The body steered him towards the door. He felt the pressure of cold steel on the back of his head. There was no choice what to do now, so he gathered his thoughts and decided to say that he had arrived per the instructions given and was checking it was the right place.

"Ah, our next guest," one of the men inside announced.

Jussi and the female form behind him entered the room. Both of the men and Heli turned to meet his gaze. Jussi looked at Heli, who smiled weakly at him. He could feel the gun move slowly down from his head to his back and then pushed in with slightly more pressure. He was guided towards a chair near Heli. This gave him a view of the person who had forced him into the cabin. He was surprised to see a slim, attractive woman with long, dark, straight hair smiling at him. The other two men were both short in height, with one of them being decidedly stockier.

Jussi was directed to sit down on one of the wooden chairs, and one of the silent men restrained him with a cable tie. Jussi presumed that Heli was tied with a similar restraint.

"Thank you for coming, Jussi," one of the men said in a quiet voice.

Although he spoke in English, Jussi deduced this accent was Finnish.

The girl moved towards them and asked, in a clear and measured Russian accent:

"We have a simple deal on the table for you both. You will give us something, and we will give you something in return. Do you understand?"

She paused for effect and then continued.

"All you need to do is tell us where the other paintings are, and we will release you. I assume your car is parked nearby, Jussi? You can then walk to the car with Heli and leave. We will soon be gone, and this will all be over. Now, tell us the location of the other paintings."

"What paintings? What are you talking about? I don't have any paintings," Jussi blurted out.

He was confused at first, but then a moment later, he realised that she must be talking about 'The Paintings of Rauma'.

"Are you talking about the painting that was stolen from the museum?" he asked.

"Yes. And now we want the others."

"All I know is there have been some paintings stolen, and there have also been two murders, which may or may not be connected. Is that what this is all about? Do you have something to do with it?"

"I will ask the question again. Where are the other paintings? We know that you and your girlfriend have been very busy researching everything. So, why don't we avoid any unnecessary unpleasantness, especially towards her and get to the point? We need the other paintings, and I don't intend to repeat my question."

Jussi answered, "I don't know what you mean. I don't know where any of these paintings are. I know there is some connection between them, but you are way ahead of me. If you know where they are, I would be interested to know. I also suggest that if you have something to do with the crimes connected to these paintings, that you hand yourself in to the police."

"You don't know what I mean? Why don't I believe you, Jussi?" the woman asked.

"I have no idea where they are. If I did, don't you think I would trade some old paintings that are not worth anything for Heli's safe release?"

"What did the journalist tell you?" she asked, very calmly but firmly.

Jussi was surprised she knew about his visit to Ms Korhonen.

"Just that there were some old paintings of Rauma, commissioned for an anniversary of the city. They were sold by the museum later on. You haven't done anything to Ms Korhonen, have you?"

"No, we're not interested in her, but we are interested in the paintings, Jussi. One last time: where are they?"

"I have no idea, really. I could lie but that would be pointless."

Jussi noticed her look at the men and nod her head. He was grabbed around the chest by one man, and his sleeve was pulled up by the other. He felt the sharp jab of a needle and struggled for a few seconds but soon began to feel weaker. Heli already had her eyes closed.

"What's happening? What have you done to us?" he asked drowsily.

"Don't worry, nothing bad is happening. You will wake up later on with a small headache. Things could be worse - much, much worse."

Jussi felt the room was closing in on him and despite his fighting, his vision gradually blurred into darkness.

No sooner had he lost consciousness - Jussi awoke again.

He opened his eyes and looked around the room. Heli was asleep in the chair opposite him, and there seemed to be no one else present. He felt his arms and was able to move them; he was not restrained anymore. He rose quickly and then wished he hadn't, as the room started to spin and he was forced to sit down again immediately. He had the feeling of something pressing down on his head from inside. He groaned and, after a moment, when his vision cleared, slowly rose to his feet again. He staggered over to Heli and felt her forehead. She was warm and presumably alive.

"Heli, wake up!"

She slowly opened her eyes, which dilated and gradually recognised him. She smiled and started to get up, starting to roll the chair forwards as she did so. She tried to speak but couldn't.

"It's alright, take it easy. Let's wait a moment. We seem to be alone now."

Jussi steadied her chair. They sat in silence for a few moments: Heli in her chair and Jussi semi-kneeling on the floor.

After a while, they both felt like moving.

"Do you feel okay to walk?" Jussi asked.

Heli nodded slowly.

"So, let's get the hell out of here!"

She nodded again, and while supporting each other, they staggered out of the door and onto the terrace.

Jussi didn't know whether any of their captors were still around or somewhere on the road, but he wasn't taking any chances. They moved quickly off the terrace and into the pitch darkness of the forest. They walked for a few minutes and kneeled to see if they could see anyone - just as Jussi had done earlier; the silence and darkness were welcome once now.

Satisfied they were safe, at least to some extent, they made their way back around the lake on a similar route to that already taken by Jussi. This time, it took a little longer as they stopped to rest and check their surroundings at frequent intervals.

Eventually, they made it back to the car. However, not until Jussi had thoroughly inspected the vehicle to ensure that things were normal. They dived into it and he hit the central locking button, turned the key, and the engine roared into life. He pressed the accelerator and almost flew out of the forest along the dirt track, swerving back onto the main road within minutes.

Having time to think now, he felt his pockets and gun holster and noted the torch and gun were surprisingly still there. However, his mobile phone was missing.

The couple drove in the direction of the police station in Rauma, at some speed.

AN INVESTIGATION

It was to be a long morning at the police station.

Jussi and Heli recounted their previous night's adventures to Jussi's colleagues in as much detail as possible. The other officers sat with incredulous expressions across their faces, hardly able to believe what they were hearing.

Jussi and Heli had already prepared. They had discussed the whole chain of events during their drive to Rauma. When they had arrived at the station, Jussi wrote everything down on paper, so when the Inspector walked in, they could walk her through the details. He was nervous about the prospect of doing so, though, as he knew that despite a safe rescue, he had broken some rules along the way.

During this process, he found his superior, Maarit, apparently unavailable, so they completed their report together with Jussi's colleagues.

Later that morning, Jussi and Heli were so tired that they decided to return to the apartment. They hadn't slept all night, so they ate a sandwich, went to bed and immediately fell asleep.

◆ ◆ ◆

Jussi had expected to have a long sleep, but to his surprise, he awoke just four hours later. Moving his head to one side, he noticed Heli was fast asleep. He was still tired but decided that he wouldn't be able to sleep again, so he sidled out of bed and walked softly to the kitchen. He had a thick annoying headache which he put down to whatever drug he had been given at the cabin.

Was it something to get information about the paintings? Or just a sleeping drug? he wondered.

He didn't know. Right now, his coffee machine was calling to him, so he switched it on and spooned in some coffee beans. His house was quite old, and the small kitchen was in a small separate room, so the noise of bubbling coffee wouldn't wake Heli.

When it was ready, he poured himself a generous cup and sat down at the small table. He began running over the events of the previous night again in his head. The more he thought about them, the more he couldn't believe what had happened, and to him, a Police Officer.

Kidnapping, guns, unanswered questions, to which he didn't know the answers, and then being drugged and let go - Why? So much of the puzzle was connected, but so much of it didn't make sense. The mug of coffee slowly began to affect Jussi, and he munched a cereal bar as he pondered the facts once again.

Of course, he had known there was a connection between the paintings. All the kidnappers had done was make that connection more concrete. It felt like they had told him more than he had told them.

Why would they do that? He asked himself, after pouring another mug of coffee.

It was while Jussi was pondering this question that the door opened, and Heli walked in.

"Ah, coffee! Where's mine?"

Jussi smiled and poured her a cup of his extra-strong morning brew.

"Wow, this should wake me up," she smiled after taking a small sip.

After greeting her, he explained his thoughts about the previous night and what had been going through his mind.

"I could guess why they let us go," Heli remarked.

When prompted by Jussi, she explained that it seemed their teamwork had found out more than the gang had done. Could it be that they had discovered so much, the gang had wanted them to fill in the gaps? But why? In addition, it was also highly possible that the gang members were guilty of theft and murder.

"They had to have known that we would involve the whole police force after the kidnapping - wasn't it a huge risk?" Jussi questioned.

He had an appointment with Maarit, his Inspector, later that day. He wanted to use the time he had beforehand to best effect. He wasn't looking forward to the meeting. Although he could see more progress being made, he expected some criticism and a reprimand for going off on his own.

I probably deserve it, he thought. *I put my own life and possibly Heli's life in danger too.*

Again, they decided to run through everything they had and made notes on pieces of paper, stating: Murder of Artist, Painting Stolen, and so on. They laid the papers onto the table to try and solve the puzzle.

The conversation took them towards the next logical step in the process. The answer to the puzzle must lie in finding the remaining 'Paintings of Rauma' and apprehending the criminals involved; this might wrap up multiple cases in Finland. Jussi took his laptop, and they concentrated on locating the other paintings.

The lady, Emma Korhonen, had stated that the murdered artist had kept one of the paintings, and another had been at the museum in Rauma. Possibly, the gang had thought that there were more pieces in the museum, as it had been broken into twice. At least one of the paintings had been at the farm where the owner had been murdered. Also, one or more could be in Helsinki, according to the journalist. In the absence of any more clues, Helsinki should be the next destination to search.

After a couple of hours of research, Jussi felt more prepared, and was ready to present his case to his superiors at the station. He put on his uniform, with particular attention to detail, and left the house into the cold morning air. In the meantime, Heli promised to get some more sleep. He left her there, sprawled contentedly in his old easy chair, by the fire.

The first part of the meeting didn't go quite as well as Jussi had hoped. To say that he received a severe dressing-down would be an understatement. The conversation was entirely one-way and referred directly to his communication shortcomings. The discussion improved when he explained his theory and visually mapped out the facts, just as he had done with Heli at his house.

During the meeting, Pekka, knowing some of the facts of the case, knocked and entered the room. He brought news that the Kiasma Gallery in Helsinki had been broken into and a single painting stolen. The theft had been by a little-known Finnish Artist: Stefan Hämäläinen.

"That's it!" said Jussi. "This is now as clear as day. This gang are obviously looking for the whole series of paintings. They may even have them all now. We just don't know why?"

He thought for a moment: *How did they know the paintings were in Helsinki? Of course, there are, or were, probably some of the pictures there - but how could they have found out?*

His thoughts wandered back to the possibility of a truth drug being used on him, back at the cottage.

"Right!" Maarit announced, clearly with her Inspector's hat on.

"Now, Jussi, I want you to put anything else down on paper, attached to your first report, so we have all of the facts together. We will circulate it across Finland and flag it up to the police forces involved in these connected cases. I want a conference with the key people involved in them today. We need to determine what our strategy should be. Somewhere, we must have CCTV footage, witness accounts, DNA and anything else that might point to these criminals - if some are Russian, then it narrows down the search."

Everything sprang into action as more of the station personnel became involved. Telephones began to ring, emails were sent, and schedules started to fill.

In the meantime, Jussi called to Emma Korhonen and was relieved to find her safe and well. In fact, she had received no contact from anyone on the matter since Jussi. He asked her to decline any proposed meeting or unknown callers, and if this happened, to report it to the local police immediately. He then contacted the police in Laitila to request them to pass by her home and check on her. A conference call with the police forces involved was arranged to shape a combined task force.

Later that day, in the meeting room at the station were: Jussi, Harri, Pekka, Maarit, and a detective from Pori named Juhani. Also networked in on the call, were personnel from police stations in both Helsinki and Närpiö.

After much discussion, for the best part of two hours, a plan was outlined and agreed upon.

As there were possibly no more paintings to find, the focus

would be on research. They would view CCTV images and look for hotel bookings or credit card trails to identify the gang and their location. Once they had a face or a name, they could mobilise a full search.

It was a busy day in the office but without any updates concerning the crimes. Plenty of research had been completed, but they had yet to find something concrete to lead them to the perpetrators. Some of the team continued working, while the rest took a break and left the station.

It had been a long day, and Jussi walked home, satisfied that he was doing his job and had a plan to progress. They were moving forward now, and through his research - he may even have redeemed himself to Maarit.

He was even happier to step back into his apartment, where he found Heli cooking a beef and vegetable casserole, which smelled delicious. He swiftly opened a bottle of red wine from the cabinet, poured two generous glasses and sat down with her to eat.

Following dinner, they both sank into his sofa, linked in each other's arms, and talked through the day's events. It wasn't long before Heli fell asleep.

Jussi stayed awake, having decided to set up a location-finder application on his mobile phone. He would link it to Heli's phone the next day - he was determined for her not to be in danger again.

THE NUMBERS

The gang's current accommodation was one of those ugly seventies buildings that should never really have been built. After the war, as in other countries, Finland had to construct such purpose-built houses out of necessity rather than design. Grim would be a suitable word to describe the style of the building, but it suited their purposes.

Inside, the house was sparsely furnished. There was an old fireplace with a fire gently burning in the hearth. Around the room were several paintings displayed side-by-side against old striped wallpaper; five paintings in all. The rest of the room contained a few random chairs and a pile of junk in one corner, removed from the walls and stacked to make room for the temporary gallery. There was also a range of bottles, mostly vodka, sitting on a table in the room's centre.

The five paintings depicted a series of scenes from the old town of Rauma, which included: the old town square, the church with a tall spire, a long, very narrow, cobbled street, a perspective of the canal running through the town, and an old wooden house alone by the sea. Although the pictures were of quite different subjects, they were clearly part of a series by the same artist and in the same area - due to the similar style, colours and shades used.

The paintings were particularly impressive when grouped, and there had been a discussion about why they had been separated and ended up in different parts of Finland. It had undoubtedly made locating them much more complicated and time-consuming.

There had also been many conversations about the location of the missing sixth painting. The whereabouts of that one remained a mystery. Had this group been interested in art, they might have tracked down these buildings. They may even have walked the streets to observe and compare them with the paintings, noting how the artist had brought them to life on canvas. However, they were not interested in art. It was a very different matter of interest that was in discussion at that moment.

The members of the gang stood in the living room, looking at the paintings with thoughtful expressions. Sabrina Nazarova, a slim, attractive woman, was scowling at one of the paintings as if it had just insulted her. She wore a gold and black Versace jumper and tight black leggings with a glass of ice-cold Stolichnaya vodka in her right hand. She swiftly drank it, slammed it down on the table and began walking up and down once more in their newly created gallery.

The other two men wore jeans and dark jumpers and stared alternately at the paintings and Sabrina. They were Oleg and Stanislav, partners with Sabrina in this project. However, it was clear who the gang leader was, and Sabrina wore the title with ease.

They spoke Russian together, although Sabrina and Oleg were quite proficient in Finnish and English. Stanislav's language skills were limited, and he only spoke Russian. Sabrina was a linguist from St. Petersburg, with no known criminal past but with a strong penchant for manipulation and an even stronger thirst for wealth. Oleg was a well-travelled criminal, with a somewhat murky past, from within various Russian intelligence services. Stanislav was a career criminal - the muscle, as he was sometimes described.

Sabrina turned around and began to pace the room.

"Why don't you just sit down and have another drink Sabrina?" suggested Oleg.

The look that Sabrina shot back clearly expressed her feelings towards him, and he raised his eyes to the ceiling and sighed as she did the same, only louder. Stanislav smiled to himself. They were already accustomed to Sabrina's mood swings.

"I don't understand," Sabrina went on. "We have five of the paintings. We believe the other may be somewhere in Helsinki, but we've found nothing to provide us with its location, and these paintings are not telling us anything!"

"Could the place we're looking for be somewhere in Rauma?" Stanislav suggested. "Could these paintings be somehow connected to one point in the town? Or would that be too obvious?"

Sabrina went on, "It's possible. Or could it be some anagram made up of the buildings? Or should we rip them up and look for a secret map?" she laughed. "Or could the fifth painting be the only one that has the real clue to the valuables' location?"

They went on manufacturing theories during the evening while Sabrina continued to pace the floor. They decided that the obvious thing to do was remove the paintings from their frames and check them thoroughly. However, it had taken a long time to track the pictures down, and they had taken considerable risks to do so. Therefore, they had been reluctant to damage them in any way, lest it may cloud the solution to the mystery or somehow devalue the final prize itself.

Sabrina took the lead as usual.

"Let's go through the facts again. In 1917, at the beginning of the Russian revolution, a small group of tsar loyalists were tasked with removing treasure from the royal palaces to hide in a safe place for when the need arose. Some of the valuables were hidden in a place where only one man knew their location, who faithfully kept the secret until his death."

She took a breath before continuing.

"According to his instructions, to ensure the location wasn't lost forever, he was to pass it on to a highly trusted associate, which he did. He told a local artist, who took the directions for the location and split them into six separate places, so not even he would know where the site was. Then, each instruction was included within a series of pictures he painted called: 'The Paintings of Rauma.' He never received a call to action during his life. Subsequently, He went to his grave, revealing only the name of the series of paintings to the next trustee."

Another breath.

"Fast forward to now, thanks to some good information; we have discovered most of the paintings that still exist. And here we are now, with nothing to show for it. Should we now remove the frames from the pictures now and begin to look at every millimetre of their canvasses? It seems there's no choice."

Stanislav and Oleg nodded in agreement.

"Da, da, da!"

They would have done this two hours ago but understood the value of Sabrina's leadership. They didn't want to do anything rash that might damage their chances of success or incur her wrath. She could say Nyet (no) in the same way that a cobra was able to spit venom. Despite both being burly and military-trained, neither wanted to be on the receiving end of an angry Sabrina.

Oleg took out a selection of tools and picked up a small scalpel as Stanislav took the first painting off the wall and laid it gently on the table. Sabrina cleared the bottles and glasses to a small side table in the corner and angled a table lamp to increase the light on the main table.

Oleg turned the painting over and carefully examined it. He had done this several times previously but wanted to be sure where he should cut and, if so - into what.

He decided the first step should be simply removing the canvas from the frame, causing as little damage as possible. He began at the top corner and slowly slid the scalpel downwards. All the while, he checked for any markings inside the fold of the canvas and on the frame itself.

Sabrina and Stanislav looked on intently, almost holding their breath as if any noise or movement would render the painting useless.

Next, he ran the scalpel along the bottom of the painting, very slowly, with a scraping noise. He opened the opposite side and the top. Finally, after a somewhat nerve-wracking few minutes, he stood back to admire his handiwork for a moment.

Oleg had sweat starting to bead on his forehead as he removed the canvas and placed it carefully next to the frame. Then, he walked around the table to their improvised bar and fixed himself a drink, pouring a top-up for the other glasses. He would need a stiff drink if this careful work were to continue with the other paintings.

After some discussion, the next stage of the operation was agreed upon. He was to work on the frame and remove its backing and then side sections. He would check in every possible place for any sign of a clue, marking, map, words, numbers or anything else outside of the usual. He worked carefully on the frame for another few minutes, but still, he found nothing.

Sabrina sighed loudly with impatience and stood up straight again. She was becoming increasingly frustrated. Oleg looked on in his relaxed and stolid manner, waiting patiently for something to happen, gently shaking his head at Sabrina's frustration.

The next stage was to check the canvas for anything hidden, or that could have been added to the canvas later.

In one corner, Stanislav noticed a tiny corner, having been folded over and stuck down. He very slowly and deftly cut away the adhesive, holding it down and lifted the corner.

There, written on the canvas, although very small, was the number 7. The gang members smiled in anticipation.

Could this be it? Could this be the key to the fortune?

It wasn't much to go on at this stage, especially as there were six paintings in the series. On reflection, they decided that this may or may not be significant as the clue could be hidden behind the paint or in another equally complex way.

They decided to take a second painting and give it the same treatment. Painting number two was of the long, cobbled street, and Oleg gently cut it away from its frame. Stanislav checked in the same place as the other frame. There it was, but this time it was the number 62. Oleg then took the third painting, the view of the canal and repeated the process.

Sabrina's mind suddenly clicked.

Without thinking, she blurted, "Could this be a map reference? If we had all six paintings, we would have a six-digit map reference."

"Did they have map references back then?" asked Stanislav.

"Yes, they've been around for centuries," Sabrina replied.

Could it be so simple and yet so obvious? they wondered.

They set about working on the other two paintings. At the same time, Sabrina booted up her laptop to check if this theory could be the key to the mystery. The other paintings revealed more digits, and when they were finished, the group surveyed the five numbers.

The other two waited in silence while Sabrina checked the numbers against the map she had found online. It was a simple job to place the numbers next to each other to form logical co-ordinates within Finland.

The map reference led her back to the small village called Urjala, on the outskirts of Rauma. It contained a few farms and some older houses clustered around a central point. The following coordinates led her to a small field near the sea. The final digits placed the location towards the end of it, near some buildings.

"Yes!" Sabrina exclaimed. "For a moment there, I thought we might be missing one of the primary coordinates, which would make it impossible to find. Now, we have it narrowed down to a field and the northern third of that field. And it's back in Urjula. So it wasn't buried so far away from the artist afterall? Finally, we have a chance of finding it, and hopefully without taking any more risks."

With that, they replenished their glasses with vodka, clinked their glasses loudly and took another drink.

"We'll check the area tomorrow," Sabrina declared, refilling her glass.

At least one bottle would be finished by the end of that evening.

GETTING CLOSER

At the police station in Rauma, Jussi's head was deep inside his laptop. It had been there for some time.

One of the challenges of police work is detailed research, which often involves trawling through masses of papers, online records and the internet. At that particular moment, it involved watching hours and hours of CCTV footage.

As Jussi had seen the gang's faces, he was the one tasked to do this visual part of the search. Heli could be called in to assist and add confirmatory evidence if needed. For now, though, it was his job.

He had been scanning the videos for several hours already, broken only by lunch. He was about to give up and take a break, when suddenly, in one of the supermarket videos, he saw what he thought was a familiar face - it was the woman. She was unmistakable in her features and dressed in black. Despite the vague definition of her figure, it was certainly her. He didn't know her name but knew she had shopped here in Rauma for something. He clipped the film section and emailed it to the technical lab to improve the definition of the picture. He then set about studying more footage.

This is what he spent much of his day doing. Still, by the end of it, he had a face at the supermarket, several times, and also at Alko, the state-owned alcohol store, where the woman seemed to be a regular visitor. He hadn't noticed any sign of the two men involved, although they were less memorable in appearance.

He called Heli on her mobile phone. She was walking through the city streets, expecting to see him soon. On receipt of his call, she was asked to make her way over to the police station and verify the images.

Once at the station, she reviewed the footage. The conclusion was that she could not be sure about the person, as she hadn't had a good look at her for any length of time. The video was also quite grainy. However, she did say that it was possibly her. This feedback gave Jussi some optimism, and he bade her farewell.

Later on, Jussi returned home. Heli had excused herself that evening to meet an old friend for dinner who lived near Rauma.

Finding himself alone, Jussi ordered a home-delivery pizza, which he ate in front of the television, and thoroughly enjoyed.

Heli arrived later, and they went for a short walk outside, before going to bed soon afterwards.

◆ ◆ ◆

The next day, Jussi resolved to follow his lead with the supermarket staff and check its credit card records.

First thing in the morning, he visited the supermarket near the centre of town to check the payment records and interview key staff. It was a large establishment, and he knew further visits might be necessary to locate the team members on duty at relevant times. At this stage, he was hoping for a breakthrough that would identify either the car, an address, or a name.

Jussi spoke to the duty manager, who provided access to the credit card records of the day. He used the time stamp from the video to check Sabrina's payment records from the till used. Of course, she had paid in cash. It would have been too easy for him to find a credit card to identify her. But he was then able to use the recorded CCTV feed and follow her into the carpark.

Her car had been parked some distance away - Jussi presumed deliberately. However, he was able to see her walk back to a grey saloon car, set back near some bushes. He arranged for someone to check the traffic CCTV feed while he interviewed the cashier who had served Sabrina: she didn't remember her.

He received a call from the station, and Pekka informed him that they had identified the suspect car on a traffic camera. It was a rented vehicle, registered at an address near Eura, around forty-five minutes away. Jussi couldn't believe his luck, and they hurriedly arranged for a team to drive to the house. If the car was there, they would enter the property with all necessary force.

Pekka arranged a squad with arms, and in addition to their service revolvers, two officers took automatic rifles. He met Jussi and they joined a convoy of three cars. Shortly afterwards, they were all speeding towards Eura.

When the team arrived close to the cottage, they left their cars blocking the road. They continued to carefully and quietly surround the address on foot. Pekka arranged for the officers with rifles to cover the house from a safe distance.

Pekka, Jussi, Harri, and four other officers from Rauma, plus two officers from Eura approached the house and settled down to wait. There was no activity, and no grey car was visible.

At Pekka's direction, two of the officers moved in closer and stood at either side of the door. Then Pekka and Jussi moved in, ready to go straight through the front door. Pekka signalled, and the other officers moved up, with one of them holding a battering ram. Then, one of the officers knocked on the door - no answer.

BANG!

They rammed open the door, and everyone rushed in with their guns at the ready. The team moved quickly through the door, covering each other as they went.

"Damn!" said Pekka looking at Jussi. "Nobody. We're too late. Let's check the rest of the house."

It didn't take long to deduce that the living room had been used as a base for the gang. Picture frames were on the floor, which was an immediate giveaway. The table with empty bottles of vodka was in a corner, together with fast-food wrappers. There was no sign of any canvasses from the paintings, they had disappeared with the gang.

◆ ◆ ◆

Two hours before, the scene inside the house had been very different.

The three members of the gang were eating a simple breakfast of bread rolls, cheese, orange juice and coffee. The conversation at the table centred on the location of what they now referred to as 'the treasure'.

The men discussed visiting a hardware store and buying digging tools. They would need spades, trowels, a hammer, a pick-axe, drill, screwdrivers and other useful implements.

Would they need explosives too? they wondered.

Sabrina disagreed and said that for all they know, the treasure could be underwater or inside a house and they should check the area first to plan next steps. The men agreed, and it was decided they would drive to the site and look around later that day without making things look suspicious to any observers. They could then purchase the necessary tools and provisions. The gang planned to return under cover of darkness, and do what was necessary.

Shortly after their conversation, and when they had finished eating, Sabrina's telephone rang. She stood up, walked around and uttered some affirmatives while the caller presumably imparted some information. She then closed her phone.

"We have to go!" she exclaimed.

"When?" Stanislav asked.

"Right now, the police are coming!"

The gang sprang into action, clearing all of the essential items into a large bag, including the unopened bottles of vodka. Sabrina rolled the canvasses and placed them carefully into a suitcase.

Within ten minutes, everything was packed into the car's boot. The gang jumped in and Oleg simultaneously floored the accelerator. The car sped down the long drive and onto the main road, driving in the opposite direction from Rauma.

"Let's drive for an hour and get well away from here," Sabrina directed, already deep in her mobile phone. "I'll find a place on the internet that we can rent for a couple of days until things die down. Then we can get back to work."

They disappeared into the distance, with Oleg now driving at the speed limit, at Sabrina's strict instruction. She didn't want them to be stopped at a random speed trap or snapped by a speed camera.

Therefore, it was an empty house that the police staked out and stormed that morning. Jussi couldn't believe how unlucky they had been.

The breakfast plates and provisions were laid out - even the coffee pot was still warm; they had just missed them.

The police taped off the area and called in forensics experts to check for any helpful evidence. In addition, the two officers from Eura remained to stake out the house from a distance, just in case of the remote eventuality of the gang returning. The rest of the team drove back, disappointedly, to Rauma.

Sabrina had already found a suitable location. She chose one of the many isolated cottages in the area that could be rented online; a holiday rental in another forested area by a lake. She decided not to travel too far, in case patrols were looking for them on the road. They reached the cottage in less than forty minutes.

On arrival, they emptied the car. Oleg took some time to ensure that the vehicle was empty and meticulously wiped the upholstery and metal parts for prints. Previous experience had taught him to be careful in this regard.

After everything was removed, he drove the vehicle further into the trees and covered its bonnet with branches so it couldn't be seen from the dirt track.

In the cottage that evening, the conversation was predictable. The gang was now more concerned with their narrow escape rather than the urgency of the main task. The incident had been unexpected. Without the tip-off, they could already be languishing inside a prison cell. For some reason, the police now seemed to be just one step behind them.

"Perhaps it was unwise to let the policeman go?" Stanislav asked.

Sabrina replied with a satisfied sneer.

"He's been so useful, though, and we've received some valuable information as a result of his interest."

"We should go and check the possible location tomorrow," Oleg added. "We don't have time to waste now. How long will it be before they find this place? Or discover our real purpose?"

The others looked at him and nodded in agreement. Sabrina decided they should discontinue the use of their current car. It was probably a liability by now. They decided the easiest thing was to buy another car and leave this one in the forest. They could have stolen another vehicle, but they didn't want to raise any more suspicion about what they were driving, nor leave any rental records. Besides, they still had more than enough money to do everything they needed and then leave Finland for good.

That morning, Sabrina dropped Oleg off in a nearby village, where he took a taxi to Tampere. He visited a car dealership with a bag containing a sizeable amount of cash. He selected a suitable vehicle: a higher mileage performance saloon. It wasn't cheap, but the prime importance was for it to be fast enough to get them out of trouble.

After road-testing and inspecting under the bonnet, Oleg was satisfied. He negotiated some new winter tyres, made a deal, paid, and then drove speedily back to the cottage in the newly-purchased vehicle.

They ate bags of fast food at the cottage that Oleg had picked up on his return journey from a burger place near the airport. After this, he spent another half an hour covering their previous car with more branches.

By early afternoon, they were ready to move and headed towards Urjala. Oleg enjoyed his drive in the replacement car and was happier to have something better than before. It made him feel considerably more comfortable with its potential for acceleration and speed, in case he might need it. Once again, at Sabrina's insistence, he had been careful to maintain the speed limit, as there were many speed cameras in the area.

He pulled off the main road onto a minor road that took them further towards the sea, although due to the number of farms and cottages around, they couldn't actually see the coast.

Now, they could quickly navigate their whereabouts with a map and the five numbers out of six used for the grid reference. This led them to a smaller dirt track, which they followed, arriving at a wooded area with some decrepit outbuildings.

Looking around, they hadn't realised how large the area might be. The gang noted that if they needed to dig across such a sizeable area, they would need some heavy-duty equipment. Wheeled, motorised diggers might even be required to do the job.

They strolled around the woods, trying not to look as if they were paying too much attention to detail, just in case someone was watching them. However, they seemed to be alone; there were a couple of distant houses, but they were far enough away. Indeed, at night, they would be invisible thanks to a combination of darkness and forest. Sabrina knew the outbuildings probably belonged to somebody, though.

After half an hour, she decided they had stayed long enough. They packed themselves back into the car and headed towards the rented cottage to await the fall of darkness.

Back at the station, Jussi had joined one of his other colleagues, Topias, to review more CCTV footage. He had hardly sat down when he saw something new. He couldn't believe his luck: a camera had picked up the grey car driving what must have been their getaway journey towards the city of Tampere. After they had picked out the vehicle on the video, they were able to follow it's progress for a while, but then it disappeared.

"So, we don't see the car after that shot. Could they have gone into hiding nearby?" Jussi asked.

Topias replied, "Either that or they changed their car."

This idea set them on another trail. After a fruitless search for stolen cars, they printed a list of car sales and rental outlets in the area and telephoned each one of them.

Finally, they found two possibilities that looked promising. Both deals had been completed that day. One was a BMW and the other an Alpha Romeo, having both been sold for cash.

"Either one could be it. They are both big and fast enough for what they would need," said Jussi.

He sent the information to the cars in the area. Then, as there was little else to do at that point, Jussi returned home, where he found himself alone again. Heli had left a note that she had decided to go shopping for new clothes and would see him later.

Jussi started to think about food: something easy. He called the nearby Italian restaurant for pizzas. He ordered them and was told they would both be ready in about thirty minutes.

He sat down with a coffee to read the local newspaper while he waited. Jussi was pleased to have some space again. He was accustomed to having his own time, although he did find Heli's distractions quite appealing.

THE SEARCH

It seemed an age that the gang sat and waited for night to fall. Even though, at that time of year, the nights drew in much earlier.

Oleg had purchased what tools they might need from a store during the day, together with some extra lights and powerful torches. They also packed guns. At this stage of the treasure hunt, they were determined that nobody would get in the way of what could be precious finds at the end of a difficult journey.

They donned layers of dark, warm clothing and prepared their equipment, leaving the cabin with Sabrina's instructions resonating in their heads. She had stressed how imperative it was that they didn't cause so much light as to make themselves visible. In addition, she'd warned them not to make any loud noises - and primarily not to shoot anyone, unless absolutely necessary. They couldn't risk anyone finding out what they were doing, or all could be lost.

They set off together in the car, and after forty minutes, arrived at the same location in Urjala they had visited earlier. This time, as they turned off the main road, Oleg switched off his headlights, and they slowly made their way to the relative cover of the forest.

They parked underneath the trees to remain hidden, and exited the car. Their next task was to check the outbuildings in the clearing to search for clues where the treasure might be. The team split up with partially covered torches and scoured the area carefully.

There was nothing much to see except some farm tools and an old tractor, almost rusted away. They had the distinct impression that nobody had been there in years.

At one point, Sabrina heard loud banging noises coming from one of the buildings. She immediately rushed across to it, jogging in her designer trainers.

"Shh! What the hell do you think you're doing?" she scolded.

Oleg looked up at her with a blank look and answered.

"This floor feels as if it could be hollow. Listen to this."

He banged on the floorboards again.

"Wait! Oleg!" Sabrina hissed.

She walked quickly and quietly out of the building. She was concerned about the noise they had already made, let alone any more noise they would probably need to make. Oleg followed closely behind her, removing his pistol from his shoulder holster as he did so.

"Check up the road, and also those houses for any movement or lights," she directed.

She walked around the buildings and checked the area behind the building herself, and then met up with Stanislav, who had been searching a small outhouse.

A few minutes later, Oleg met them back at the outside of the building. They agreed that nobody had been alerted by their activity, and things looked safe to progress.

After a brief discussion, as Sabrina was nervous about being seen, she directed Stanislav to position himself up the road with a clear view of the main road and distant houses. Satisfied they could now risk making more noise, Sabrina asked Oleg to continue the task. This time, he weighed into the boards with a heavy pickaxe.

Bang! Bang! Bang!

Oleg was a short but powerful man, and the building shook as he struck the floor. Within ten minutes, he had broken through it. Underneath, there seemed to be another floor. He looked at Sabrina, his face asking to continue, to which she nodded. She had a feeling they might have to do this in all of the buildings. She was also concerned that someone might discover their handiwork in the morning if they were not successful tonight. Sabrina sincerely hoped nobody had visited the place in years.

Bang! Bang! Bang!

This time Oleg attacked the floor with more force. The old floorboards began to splinter, and together they removed and threw them to the far end of the room, revealing a large hole in the ground, big enough for someone to drop into.

"Stop for a while now," instructed Sabrina.

She walked out of the building and quickly up the road towards Stanislav. She trusted him to do what was necessary to secure their project, no matter what. Both Stanlisav and Oleg had their skills but couldn't perform each other's tasks competently. That's why they needed a leader to delegate the right jobs. Sabrina was the perfect mix of intellect and guile, mixed with her overwhelming sense of authority.

"Is everything still okay, Stanislav?" she asked.

"Yes, not a sound and all the lights are still out. I think the people in those houses are either too far away or just too old and too deaf."

Sabrina smiled and continued, "Good. This could be an interesting place, although I would be surprised if we were so fortunate straight away. Now that we've started digging, let's dig all night if needed, so get comfortable."

Stanislav nodded in agreement.

Sabrina continued, "Stay here and out of sight. Call me if anything happens. If something does, we'll stop immediately and come to you with guns ready. If you have to shoot anything, please use a silencer. In case of emergency, the rally point is the car."

Stanislav nodded. When Sabrina was far enough down the lane, he decided to risk another cigarette without her seeing him.

Back inside, Oleg had already lowered himself into the hole, and he gestured to Sabrina to move closer. With a torch, he indicated a tunnel, extending far back in the direction of the road.

"Well, there's only one way to find out if we've been lucky first time!" Sabrina said.

She grabbed more torches and placed her phone on silent vibrate, in a pocket that would keep it tight to her body so she would feel it ring.

Oleg began to crawl forward into the tunnel. Sabrina lowered herself into the hole and shone her two torch lights past him, trying to provide as much light as possible. Oleg grunted as he crawled through the tunnel. He was not a tall man, but his width made it difficult to move. Mangled tree roots spread around the tunnel, which scraped him as he moved, covering him with small dirt-falls and annoying scratches.

At one point, Oleg found the way ahead partially blocked. He had to scrabble through the space, layering the dirt around and behind him, spreading it as flat as possible. The thought of a cave-in made him uncharacteristically nervous. At this stage, though, he decided that going forwards was probably easier than going backwards; there was no way he could turn. He could also feel a slight descent that didn't fill him with any more enthusiasm about the tight space he was in. Sweat covered his brow, and breathing was not as easy as it had been at the top; he was beginning to get concerned about the amount of air available.

As he continued, his headlight and torch illuminated a larger space, appearing in front of him.

"Thank God for that!" he exclaimed.

Oleg heaved himself through a smaller gap and arrived into an open space about four metres square. Oleg sat down for a few moments to rest while he took in his immediate surroundings.

At least I'll be able to turn around for the return journey.

As he surveyed the room, he noted it was partially boarded. Everything was kept together with thick wooden posts, designed to strengthen the walls and ceiling to prevent the earth from caving in. The room was of rudimentary construction but had stood the test of time surprisingly well. There were some wooden boxes heaped in the corner with a couple of old rifles stood against them.

Perhaps this is part of some old war defences? Or a storage place? Or even an emergency room for the farm owners? Oleg wondered.

He crawled over to the boxes and cracked one open with a chisel lodged in his belt. It didn't take much effort with Oleg's strong hands to rip off the wooden planks.

Inside the box were gun cartridges. He opened another of them, which seemed to contain perished foodstuffs, with Russian labels on them. He noted what could have been pickled beetroot.

It feels just like home, he smiled to himself.

He picked up one of the guns and inspected it. It was an old single-shot rifle. He checked another couple of boxes of similar content, which seemed to have almost disintegrated. There were papers of some kind in one of them, which had degraded into mush and were now completely unreadable.

He sat down, disappointed, and wondered about the planks that secured the room's sides and roof. He examined them to see if there was anything hidden or even hollow. He also checked the floor to see if there could be something buried underneath.

I may as well check the place thoroughly. This place is far too good a find, not to be more interesting.

After a few minutes, Oleg discovered a hollow in one of the walls and removed one of the boards. He was nervous that the whole room might cave in, and if that happened he wouldn't stand much of a chance as he was a few metres below ground.

As he pulled the board away, his headlight illuminated a space. He reached in and felt something. He grasped whatever it was and pulled out the remains of a soft leather bag. He opened it carefully, reached in, and found a small wooden box inside. On opening the clasp, what he saw inside made his heart almost miss a beat: it was a mauve-coloured egg, with tiny jewels spread across it. He gently turned it over and read the signature underneath: Peter Karl Fabergé. Oleg closed his eyes and opened them again in disbelief. He was looking at an object worth tens of millions of euros. Then, he laughed - he couldn't help it. After such a long and painful search for anything of value, he had found it in the first place they had looked.

Suddenly, there was a sound from the other end of the tunnel, and it occurred to him that Sabrina couldn't hear anything nor know what was happening. It briefly occurred to him to hide the egg again and tell her he hadn't found anything. He decided that she was too clever for that and was the only one who would have the right contacts to sell it for a high price anyway. Besides, he had developed a soft spot for her.

He decided to check inside the hole once more and felt around the wood-panelled walls inside. His hand contacted several more small cloth bags, and he gently removed them one by one.

After a few minutes of careful opening, he was surrounded by a selection of gold coins, jewellery and small statues of gold and glass; a real treasure hoard.

Oleg removed his jacket, gathered up the objects and made a makeshift bag out of it. It didn't matter to him if his coat got dirty now - he could afford many more in the future. He smiled to himself and thoroughly checked the hole and surrounding area once more.

Satisfied to have found everything of value, at least within easy reach, he shuffled around to begin his return journey. He made his way back down the tunnel, moving faster than before, despite it rising back upwards.

Eventually, he found the light of Sabrina's torch. Even though it was hard going, somehow, it felt much easier. He couldn't wait to tell her what he had found, and he also couldn't wait to find out what the possible value of the treasure might be.

When he returned to the tunnel's opening, Sabrina stepped back out of it, took a cigarette and lit it. She was getting cold and irritable as she had been stooping over the opening for some time. This was not an everyday activity for her, and her patience wasn't holding out well.

"Well, did you find anything?" she asked keenly as she blew smoke out of her nose.

Oleg smiled and opened his jacket out onto the floor. He laid out his discoveries and proudly displayed the hoard in front of her. Sabrina could hardly speak. She checked the remaining bags and felt the various objects inside before pulling each one out and describing it in turn. When she found the egg inside the walnut and jewel-encrusted box, a huge smile spread across her face as she mouthed one word: 'Faberge'.

Suddenly, Sabrina was jerked back to reality by the cold and the fact that they were in a place of some risk. Now they had discovered this hoard, the risk was even more significant. It also occurred to her that there could be more articles in the area.

Should they push their luck? Or should they quit while ahead? she considered.

She made up her mind quickly.

"Let's fill the hole," she instructed.

Sabrina and Oleg filled the hole with whatever they could find. They layered the wooden boards back on top, so it would look as if the floor had partly caved in through deterioration.

Sabrina thought, *Anyway, I can buy this place later and survey it at my leisure.*

They proceeded to remove all traces that they had ever been there; packing up the treasure, tools, lights and weapons, then putting them into the car. If there were more valuables here, then it was for another time. What they had already discovered was enough to last them for a long time - probably for the rest of their lives.

When everything was ready, Sabrina instructed Oleg to bring Stanislav back. It had also occurred to her that she could leave the two men and drive away. Still, she felt she might need their protection for some time yet, especially their guns, if something were to happen during their escape from Finland.

Besides, she thought, *they are not the type to forget a double-cross easily.*

Right now, they all seemed to trust each other, as fragile as their relationship based on crime was.

Oleg returned to Sabrina with an excited Stanislav. They got into the car and drove away into the night, noting with satisfaction that there were still no lights in the houses they passed.

Arriving at the main road, headlights were switched on, and the accelerator pressed down.

When they returned to the cabin, Sabrina carefully laid out the evening's discoveries. The items formed a valuable hoard. It included: twenty-seven solid gold coins, two small glass statues, five small gold statues, three pieces of jewellery containing emeralds and diamonds, plus the most amazing find of all - a single Fabergé egg.

Even without the egg, the rest of the items were worth millions. However, Sabrina was most interested in the egg and spent that evening researching on the internet. It didn't take long for her to discover that the egg was the missing 'mauve egg.'

On opening it, she found it contained nothing. However, further research noted that it had initially included miniature portraits of the Russian royal family - these had already been found without the egg itself.

The next piece of research she did was on the potential value. She discovered that, based upon similar valuations, this egg could be worth well over ten million dollars. Together with the rest of the treasure, the haul could make them between fifteen and twenty million dollars.

Finally, everything has been worth the effort, she smiled to herself.

She spent the rest of the evening sending several emails to potential buyers, using a secure VPN to block her location. She smiled as she typed, with anticipation of their replies.

The message contained a statement that would attract many potential buyers:

We have discovered the missing Fabergé Mauve Egg.

She shared some of her findings with the others, naturally underestimating the value.

At the end of her research, she pulled a bottle of ice-cold vodka from the fridge and announced it was time to celebrate. Tomorrow they would plan their exit and look forward to spending their rewards.

BACK TOGETHER

Jussi was worried. Heli had still not returned, and there was only so much shopping that could be done in Rauma; especially considering it was evening and she was alone. He called her mobile phone again and left a message to the effect that she should call him immediately, and that there was pizza waiting.

After a while, he ate a slice, took his coat and left the apartment to look for her. He spent an hour walking around town, asking in shops, and leaving messages on her phone, before he decided to call the station and inform the rest of the team. This resulted in an alert being sent to all available cars, and Jussi began to fear the worst.

Why is she missing for a second time? Could she have been kidnapped again?

There was a knock at the door of the cabin, and Sabrina told everyone to be silent. The gang members removed their guns from hiding places and sought cover.

The door opened, and in walked Heli.

Sabrina welcomed her: "Our fourth team member finally returns. Welcome to the party, Heli!"

"So, can I see it?" she asked excitedly. "This is either what we've been looking for, or I need to get back to Jussi before he misses me."

"I think maybe you don't need to see that particular policeman again. He's helped us as much as he can without even knowing it. Now Heli, Come and feast your eyes on this!"

Sabrina gestured to the table and opened the fabric cloths to demonstrate the treasures inside.

"Oh my God! This looks very promising. And the value?" asked Heli, as she handled the various artefacts carefully.

"I think in total, ten million dollars, so hopefully you should all receive at least a million dollars each, depending on our buyer," announced Sabrina.

"Or more? This is a Fabergé! Some of these eggs fetch a lot more than you think. It could even be tens of millions. I can't believe this is a real Fabergé - one of the missing eggs! Right, that's it, I'm staying with you, give me a glass," announced Heli.

Oleg handed her a glass and poured a generous amount of vodka into it. Heli enjoyed the drink quickly and slammed the glass down on the table.

Sabrina continued, "Now down to business for a moment. I suggest we all stay here this evening and plan our exit for tomorrow. There's no rush, we have a few days left on this rental, and the worst thing we could do right now would be to make a run for it and screw things up."

"I agree," said Stanislav. If this stuff needs to lay low for a few months, we've lost nothing, although I'm sure that we would all like to get our hands on some serious money and fly to a beach as soon as possible."

Everyone nodded, smiling. Oleg turned to Heli.

"And the policeman? Jussi? He still doesn't suspect anything? Is he stupid or something?"

"Oh no, he's not stupid," replied Heli. "I'm just really, really good, in all kinds of ways."

She winked at him. Sabrina laughed an evil laugh and poured the team another round of drinks.

◆ ◆ ◆

Back in Rauma, as nothing had turned up about Heli, Jussi was becoming increasingly concerned.

Why would they have kidnapped her again? What would be the point? They've just narrowly missed being apprehended. Why risk it? What would they have to gain?

These and other questions went through Jussi's mind. He had no answers, though, and neither did anyone else at the station. It just didn't make any sense.

It was sometime later, with no contact or progress made in the mystery, that Jussi eventually went home to try and get some rest.

After a sleepless night, he spent the morning at the station going through any possible leads or connections to the incident the day before - but he found nothing.

Should I wait for some contact from the kidnappers? he wondered.

The team at the station were sympathetic, and despite his possibly poor choices early on in the investigation, it was evident that someone Jussi cared for was in danger. Everyone put their effort into brainstorming and researching any possible leads that could help find her.

◆ ◆ ◆

At the cabin, the gang sat around a heavy old table with fresh coffee and discussed their plans. Sabrina started as usual.

"Okay, I've already sent some messages to the buyers, and we have serious interest, but they need to see the pieces - especially the egg. I prefer to get out of Finland as soon as possible. It's starting to feel too risky, and I don't want to take any risks now we have the merchandise."

The team pitched in to the discussion from various directions.

"There's a risk in flying out of the country, as our photographs may be at the airport already. The scanners may also pick up some readings from this stuff when we take it through customs," said Oleg.

"Why don't we take the ferry as we originally discussed? We could go to Estonia and meet the buyers in Tallinn. In Estonia, it's much easier to move onwards, in any number of directions," proposed Heli.

"Well, it's possible, but I'm still nervous about the amount of attention we're beginning to attract. Why not drive north, get to Tornio and cross the border where there's little security?" proposed Sabrina.

"I have to say I prefer that idea," said Stanislav. "We can meet them further inside Sweden. Once the financial business is completed, we can split up and leave in different directions. If we do it quickly, there's less risk of them realising we're leaving the country. Let's face it. They still think that we are looking for more of those damn paintings!"

Back at his apartment, Jussi remembered that Heli's mobile phone could still be trackable, if it were turned on? Some days ago, he had insisted on it. He had even helped her to install the function. Now, he was wondering if it could still be working.

He checked his phone and felt a rush of adrenalin as he saw it showing on the map. He quickly took a screenshot, just in case the reception was lost or suddenly switched off.

Jussi rushed outside, on his way, grabbing a few essentials, including a torch, his gun, a padded jacket, a good pair of gloves and a couple of cereal bars.

He drove off into the day, which was cold but fresh. The sun was turning everything brighter and whiter, with added sparkle from the snow and ice. However, given the circumstances, Jussi failed to appreciate the scene entirely, but at least it made for good driving weather. He drove quickly along the main road, taking the opportunity to overtake whenever he could.

His instinct was to call for backup, but he still didn't want to take any risks where Heli was concerned. He knew he needed to be smarter this time, though. So he decided to continue driving towards her location, and when he was closing in, call the station and ask for help. No doubt backup would be necessary, and while they were on their way, he would have time to check things out, formulate a plan, and possibly even rescue her. He had learned his lesson the first time, and was not going to go near Heli without knowing where every gang member was.

By this time, the gang in question had decided their next move and packed the essentials into the car. Stanislav had exchanged their mobile phones with a new set of pre-paid ones. While doing so, he noted that Heli had a regular phone and replaced it, destroying the other one in the process. She had forgotten about the tracking app that Jussi had made her install., but that was now useless. Stanislav also took all of the sim cards, paintings, papers and maps that he could find and threw them into the fireplace. He set a fire in the grate before leaving and watched everything burn for a few minutes until satisfied everything would be destroyed.

They got into the car and started to drive north. The journey would involve many hours of driving, between ten and twelve, with a few breaks and driver exchanges. They planned to take a variety of roads to avoid being tracked. Now they just needed to get out of Finland safely - and as fast as possible.

Jussi continued to speed towards the identified location. After an hour, he came upon the main turning, according to the map. He noted that contact had been lost with the phone but used the enlarged screenshot he took to place the approximate location back into the GPS, and he was off again.

After another twenty minutes, he swerved off the road and drove up a small track. All of his previous cautionary thoughts had disappeared. At this point, he didn't much care about backup anymore and already had a gun in his hand as he parked on the track, within sight of the cottage.

There was no sound from anywhere and nobody to be seen. He waited for what seemed like an eternity with his eyes sweeping the road ahead. He wanted to rush in, but common sense and training kept him there.

Jussi decided to call the station for help and keep the cabin covered until its arrival. After leaving the details with the desk officer, he was advised that two patrol cars from Eura were already mobile and could be with him within twenty minutes. And therefore, wisely this time, he waited.

◆ ◆ ◆

Sabrina and Heli chatted in the back of the car about potential opportunities to sell the haul. Oleg was driving, with Stanislav in the passenger seat, listening quietly to their conversation.

As they continued northwards, the weather began to change, and the sky became grey and heavy. Stanislav cursed audibly under his breath as they turned a corner to change direction, and he found himself driving head-on into the snow.

Two hours later, it was even heavier, and there seemed little chance of improvement. Oleg pushed the car forward for another hour in poor visibility. He was starting to get tired now and decided enough was enough.

"This is ridiculous! Soon we're going to end up driving off the road," he commented through gritted teeth.

"Okay, if this is as far as we can go, we need to find somewhere to stay for the night. Where are we now?" asked Sabrina.

Heli was already asleep. Stanislav scanned his smartphone for somewhere to take a break.

"We can stay in Vaasa tonight," he said. "It's only twenty to thirty minutes to the west from here."

"There are some hotels there. I'll find one for us," said Sabrina. "Find me a cashpoint on the way, and I'll spin a story to the receptionist about some problem with our Russian credit cards. We'll take two double rooms using fake names, and I'll pay cash. Everyone must speak Russian."

Heli didn't awake until they arrived at the carpark, which was thankfully underground and warm. After stretching and removing their bags, they locked the car and made their way to the reception desk via the lift.

Their story worked at reception, supported by the weather conditions, and they duly purchased their accommodation in advance.

They went to their respective rooms and dropped off their luggage. Sabrina had swapped places with Oleg, so now the girls had one room and the men the other.

Within fifteen minutes, they were back downstairs again and shown to a table in the restaurant by a young waitress who led them to a corner table. The restaurant was quiet. She left menus on the table and took their drink orders.

"Well, at least we have a warm bed, a steak and some alcohol tonight," stated Stanislav, surveying the menu.

Everyone agreed that this was the best decision, although they were still keen to get out of the country with their precious merchandise.

The waitress returned and left a bottle of vodka with glasses on the table, plus a bottle of red wine for dinner. They hit the alcohol immediately and felt themselves begin to warm up and relax. What was equally as pleasing was the arrival of the steaks. They had all ordered them, except Heli, who had gone for Salmon. The drinks were refilled, and the conversation returned to the subject of the loot.

"I know what I'm going to do with my share," announced Stanislav.

The others looked at him, smiling expectantly. "I'm going to buy a bigger apartment and upgrade my car to a big black Hummer."

"A Hummer! And where will you park that in your city?" Oleg grunted.

Sabrina laughed, "On the contrary, Stanislav, I think it's just your style. And you Heli, what'll you do?"

"I'm not sure. I'd like to go far, far away - somewhere warm. I want to move away from everything and start again. Maybe I'll buy a house on the beach with other places to rent out to people on vacation. I don't want to do anything like this again."

"Regrets about your policeman?" Sabrina asked.

"Well, I know it was the plan, but it's not so easy when you know someone, you know? I didn't agree with those deaths either. I'm sure they could've been avoided."

Oleg made an indiscernible grunt towards his glass and shot her a look.

Heli carried on regardless, "Yes, Jussi was nice, and it was a shame to do this to him, but it's too late now anyway, I guess," she smiled wanly. "I'll just have to console myself with the money."

With that comment, they all laughed.

"By the way, I have something to tell you," announced Sabrina.

"What's that?" asked Stanislav, eyeing her suspiciously.

"Don't worry, it's all good news!" she smiled.

There was a short break while the waitress returned to take the plates and ask for dessert and coffee orders.

"So....?" asked Heli when the waitress had left.

"Well, we have an offer for the merchandise. It's provisional on the items being approved as genuine, also the quality of the gold and jewels..."

She left them hanging in mid-air for dramatic effect. They all craned in towards the table, and their voices lowered, waiting for Sabrina to continue.

"Well, in total, the offer is twenty million euros. That means you will each receive two million euros each, which is even more than we thought."

Everyone was delighted with this news and clinked their glasses together in a toast. At that moment, their desserts and coffee arrived. Oleg ordered a round of congratulatory cognacs, and they relaxed into their seats with satisfaction.

Stanislav eyed Sabrina.

"So, that means fourteen million euros for you - not too bad. I wonder what you will do with all that money?"

Sabrina replied coldly, "It's not fourteen million for me, Oleg. Our sleeping partner started and financially fronted this operation. He will receive half of the total profit - that's ten million. But yes, with four million left for me, maybe I will have the money and time to buy a new outfit or two?"

"Not too bad for our mystery partner either. We take all of the risks, and he, or she, takes the lion's share of the reward," Oleg noted.

Sabrina replied, "Yes, but without him, we wouldn't have known about this in the first place. We certainly wouldn't be sitting here ready to receive our millions."

"Okay. Enough already. Let's not begrudge our mysterious benefactor," said Heli and raised her glass.

"Here's to the future - may it be brighter than any of us can imagine."

They all raised their glasses in the shared toast.

Earlier, back at the cottage, two police cars arrived. The officers jumped out of their vehicles with guns drawn. Jussi gestured for them to cover the house as he slowly made his way to the window. He glanced in, and with no activity apparent inside, gestured to one of the officers to go around the back. Then he beckoned for the others to approach and cover the doors and windows. There was no hesitation this time.

With Jussi leading the way - they ran inside, but the cottage was empty again. He couldn't believe it. For the second time in a matter of days, the gang had evaded him. There followed a cursory look around the cabin, which confirmed that nobody was there.

How is it they are always one step ahead of me? Jussi wondered.

He and the other officers dutifully searched the cottage for evidence while two officers checked outside. Jussi spotted some debris in the fireplace and combed carefully through the ashes. He found pieces of paper and canvas that had been left in the grate. Among charred pieces of canvas, were small fragments of a map, which he guessed had been used to plan the gang's escape. It was a map of Finland but didn't give any further clues. Any more investigation would have to be done by the forensics team.

At that moment, one of the local officers, Ella, strode in and informed Jussi that they had found a car hidden in the forest nearby. There had been nothing inside except some napkins, receipts and maps inside the glove compartment. She spread the items out on the table, and they went through them.

Jussi couldn't believe his luck. Two clear routes were traced on one of the maps, in thick black marker pen, one leading south to Turku and another towards Vantaa airport.

"Surely they couldn't have forgotten this? It seems too convenient," Jussi asked.

"Maybe it was deliberate?" Ella asked.

Immediately, one of the other officers called the station to have the gang members' descriptions circulated to the relevant airports.

"If they wanted to get out of the country and they know we have descriptions of them, surely they wouldn't risk the airports?" Jussi questioned.

"They could cross the border to Russia. No, too slow and risky. Or they could drive north." Ella proposed.

"As you suggested, I think this map could be a plant. I bet they'll try and cross into Russia, or else, drive north and into Sweden."

"The route with the lighter security would be Sweden. They would be able to find a way through there," Ella offered.

After more brainstorming, which led them back to the same conclusion, Jussi wrapped up the discussion. He thanked Ella, and as he did so, noted their eyes lingered on each other for a little more than they should have done. He dismissed this as he was more concerned about Heli than anything else, so he left her with a parting smile. She and the other officers remained at the scene, waiting for the forensics team.

Jussi returned to his car and opened his phone. After checking the schedule of flights northwards, he discovered he could get a flight to Oulu in about four hours. He called into the station and asked them to arrange the ticket. It was a gamble, but he decided it was a fair one, given the circumstances.

He left the cottage and set his GPS for Vantaa airport to take the flight north from there. He would liaise with the local police and airport security to check for any signs of the gang. This route would be far quicker than driving north, especially if it were poor weather. His station wired ahead to the local police in

Oulu, who would pick him up and provide assistance on arrival.

Could Jussi get one step ahead of the gang this time?

THE CHASE

The following morning, Heli awoke and opened her eyes. She looked to her side and saw Sabrina, fast asleep in the other twin bed.

Heli lay there for a while, studying the ceiling. It obviously hadn't been decorated for a while. She followed a crack across the ceiling and down the wall while she thought.

Heli had never wanted to be drawn into the criminal activity as much as she had been. When she'd been contacted about the job initially, she was attracted by the opportunity to make alot of money. The prospect of a treasure hunt had also excited her. In addition, she'd liked the idea of returning to Finland for a while and meeting Jussi again. However, things had become very complicated. Certainly, nobody was supposed to die; that had shocked her. Now, she was in so deep that there was no turning back.

Her thoughts turned to the positive side: the treasure hunt had certainly made her very wealthy. Although she would never be able to return to Finland again, she would have the money to travel or live on a beach somewhere exotic - this was something she had always dreamed of.

Heli sighed.

There was no going back now. She must look forward.

A voice interrupted her train of thought.

"What are you thinking about this morning Heli?" Sabrina asked.

Heli jumped a little.

"I was just thinking about what to do with my share of the money," she lied.

"Well, you'll get your chance soon enough. Come on, let's see if the boys are up and about."

They dressed and walked down to the breakfast room where they noticed Oleg and Stanislav, seated at the same table as they had been on the previous evening. Heli and Sabrina took some coffee from the self-service station and joined them.

"Are we ready to get across the border?" Stanislav asked.

Everyone nodded in agreement. The hotel had been an unscheduled stop, and they were all more than ready to leave the country.

After a short breakfast, they checked out of their rooms, took the lift down to the garage, stowed their bags, and started the car. Oleg began what they hoped would be their final journey within Finland, which would see them safely across the border into Sweden.

As the gang were leaving the hotel in Vaasa, Jussi's car was already tearing down the highway towards Turku. His flight was in seventy-five minutes, and with luck and speed, he should just make it in time. The weather was improving now, and even the sun had made an appearance. He felt optimistic, and the journey flew by.

Jussi arrived at the airport, arriving safely on board after an expedited passage through the terminal.

After the usual preparation, the plane took off, turned and headed north towards Oulu. He sank back in his seat and sipped coffee, puzzling over why the gang had not contacted him about Heli.

Have they really kidnapped her again? Or is she somewhere else now? If they have, perhaps they've let her go already? What use is she to them now? Or has something much worse happened?

Jussi had no answers to these questions but, in any event, was determined to find her and bring her back unscathed.

Within an hour, the plane arrived at the airport in Oulu. He marvelled at how the airport had changed since he was last there, a few years before. Gone was the functional hanger that had served as the old terminal, now replaced by a modern 21st-century airport.

After he passed security, he was pleased to find some members of the Oulu police force waiting for him. After mutual greetings, they took a seat in a café and ordered refreshments, ready to discuss strategy.

Jussi briefly explained the history to the two officers, Sampo and Petri, and then concentrated on the possible location of the fugitives. According to the map, local knowledge and some educated guesswork, they estimated they were slightly in front of the gang. They thought it would only be up to an hour at the maximum, though.

"Remember," Jussi warned. "They have weapons and are certainly dangerous. We believe at least one of them has already committed murder. Also, remember they may have an innocent female with them."

After the discussion, Petri called the station and alerted them that the gang may already be in or around Oulu. At the same time, they walked to a waiting car and took their seats. They would now drive southwards and wait for news from the other police patrols in the area.

◆ ◆ ◆

Oleg continued to drive the gang in the direction of Oulu.

"Looking at the map," Stanislav said. "If we can keep up this pace, we should pass Oulu within an hour and be in Tornio in less than another two."

"We should be able to cross the border just north of Tornio. Drive to Haparanda in Sweden, dump the car, and then take a train south. I've already arranged for us to meet the buyer in Gothenburg tomorrow evening," Sabrina announced.

Heli asked, "What about border security? Are you expecting it to be light? Don't you think they may already be looking for us?"

"Well, Tornio may have some extra police looking for four people in a car, but I doubt they'll have all our descriptions. I think we'll be fine," Sabrina replied confidently.

Oleg grunted in a non-committal fashion as he continued to press his foot down on the accelerator, heading out of danger.

"Oleg!" Sabrina rebuked him. "Do you still want us to get pulled over for speeding? That would be a little inconvenient at this point, don't you think?"

With that, he obediently decelerated to 100 kilometres per hour, smiling as he did so.

"What time are we meeting the buyer in Gothenburg tomorrow?" Heli asked.

"8 pm," Sabrina replied. "He's demanded that I go alone. You can escort me to the meeting place. I'm nervous about carrying these valuables on my own through the city."

"We'll be close. Don't worry," said Stanislav in a reassuring tone.

Stanislav didn't trust anyone these days, except perhaps Oleg. He'd known him for many years and would trust him to cover his back. However, even with Oleg, he would have to be careful. He knew the prospect of great wealth could change people, and in these situations, it was best to rely on one person and one person only: himself.

Heli looked out of the window thoughtfully. She and everyone in the car knew precisely what Stanislav meant. There was an element of companionship among the group but only to a certain point - and that point could be Gothenburg. Meanwhile, the journey was progressing well, or at least had been, until that moment.

All of a sudden, a car accelerated from the hard shoulder of the highway, and blue lights appeared, reflecting around them. A siren rang out.

"Shit!" Oleg swore.

"I told you not to go so fast," shouted Sabrina.

"I wasn't. They were waiting for us. Be quiet, all of you. I can't try and outrun them, or they'll just call in more cars. We need to get rid of them. Then we need to get off the highway and change cars - fast!"

"Pull over and let's get rid of this problem," Sabrina directed.

She reached for her pistol. Stanislav reached for his own weapon from underneath the seat. They decelerated and drew to a stop on the hard shoulder as the police car drew up close behind them. One of the officers got out.

Without warning, the two male members of the gang jumped out of the car and started shooting at the police car.

The officers were taken entirely by surprise at the speed and ferocity of the attack, and took shelter behind the side of their vehicle while drawing their own weapons.

The gang continued to fire at the car, with bullets hitting its tyres, engine and windscreen. The police car took a heavy toll as Oleg and Stanislav emptied their magazines into it - the noise was deafening.

"Now, we go!" shouted Sabrina.

The men leapt back into the car and swerved away. The officers returned fire but were too late and could only watch the gang's car speed away. They examined their patrol car briefly, saw it was hopeless to give chase, and called the station for assistance.

Oleg accelerated, and shortly their speed exceeded two hundred kilometres per hour.

After fifteen minutes of driving at this pace, he saw a road off to the right, ahead. He knew the highway would soon be closed by police cars and maybe even a helicopter, so he needed to find another way. After checking there were no other vehicles around, Oleg reduced his speed, swerved off the highway, and pressed the accelerator again. They were headed towards the coast.

Jussi was in a patrol car when the call came through from the vehicle that had intercepted the black saloon. He couldn't believe his ears, especially when he heard the shots over the radio and the frantic commentary of the officers, then more gunfire.

A message came from one of the officers:

"We've returned fire. Our vehicle is disabled, but we have no injuries. The suspect car is speeding north on highway E4."

Dispatch would arrange help for the officers while Jussi and the team sped off to try and intercept the car on the road. Other vehicles were now being mobilised, and the helicopter based in Oulu had been alerted to assist.

The gang's car was flying over the bumps in the road, and Heli held onto the door handle in an effort to steady herself. Although the ride couldn't be more uncomfortable, nobody cared. They just wanted to put as much distance between them and the police as possible. The direction was still northwards but now towards Kemi, a city some half an hour before Tornio. They were taking the back roads as Sabrina continually checked her phone for different options. Having directed Oleg to drive to a small village, they reached it within minutes and he pulled over at the train station as instructed.

"Right, it's time to dump the car," Oleg said.

Stanislav nodded.

Sabrina piped up from the rear seats, "Leave Stanislav and me here. We'll travel separately from you. You two hide the car and then join us here but don't talk to us, and make sure you use a different carriage. The next train is due in twenty-five minutes, so hurry."

They walked to the station. As it was small, there was no ticket office, but a small cafe sat on the corner. Being hungry and starved of caffeine, they decided they may as well take the opportunity to reboot their energy levels and took a seat inside.

Meanwhile, Oleg and Heli found a wooded area nearby and hid the car as best they could. Oleg commented that the police would struggle to find the car now, at least for a while. Then, they grabbed their bags and walked to the station.

The change of transport went without a hitch, and the train arrived on time. The two couples took their seats in different parts of the train, and for the first time in a few hours, felt more relaxed.

After a short journey, they arrived in Kemi, and all met in the small empty waiting room. During the trip, Sabrina had been working on her smartphone again and already developed a new plan.

"Right, it'll be a big risk crossing the border here now, so there is a private charter service at the airport. It will cost us a few thousand euros, but we should be able to charter a small plane to take us to Gothenburg, avoiding the border and the journey south."

"Sounds good to me," said Heli. "I've had enough of this road trip."

Everyone agreed, and Sabrina made a call, pacing as she did so. She returned after she'd made the call, her high-heeled boots tapping loudly on the concrete pavement.

"Right, the plane can leave within an hour. I explained we have an urgent business meeting and can't wait for the scheduled flight. The company will fly all of us there for four thousand euros, so I made the deal. Let's get to the airport."

They walked as slowly and naturally as possible, trying to behave like separate couples and allay suspicion. They took two taxis from the rank towards the airport. The private plane service was adjacent to the main terminal, with a small lounge, where they were welcomed and offered coffee. They sat nervously, half expecting some problem to appear.

They had dumped their guns in a rubbish bin in Kemi, knowing they may have to clear security somewhere. Oleg and Stanislav felt decidedly naked without their weapons, having been fully armed for the past few weeks. They had also, regretfully, disposed of the larger intricate glass vases from the treasure trove as they were not practical to hide.

Sabrina already had a specially-made case, which she had brought to Finland, with a false bottom. The hidden part of the case was covered in a unique material, which masked metals and shapes from metal detectors.

As it happened, there was almost no security at either side, except for a cursory check of their passports. After the shoot-out on the road, the rest of the getaway now seemed plain sailing.

After an uneventful flight, they took taxis into the city and arrived at the boutique hotel that Sabrina had booked. They decided to take a few hours rest before the meeting, and stayed in their rooms.

Stanislav had other plans. Having arranged to buy two replacement pistols and ammunition through an underworld contact, he met the man and returned to the hotel with the weapons. He wasn't going to take any chances until the deal was completed, and he was far, far away.

The whole police force in the north of Finland: Ostrobothnia, had been activated, but the gang's car had yet to be found. Who could have known they could so efficiently and effectively disappear?

It had been thanks to Sabrina's savvy use of her smartphone, in terms of directions, timetables and contacts, that had enabled them to switch transport and confuse the police.

It would only be later that evening that authorities would discover a flight plan for a private plane with four passengers from Kemi to Gothenburg. The Finnish police alerted the Swedish authorities, but by then, it was too late.

The gang's car was discovered a few days later in the forest; the firearms were never found.

Cooperation between the Finnish and Swedish police forces is good. The language connection assists this relationship - Swedish being the second language of Finland. Given the circumstances, it was an obvious choice to send Jussi to Gothenburg to cooperate with the Swedish police force. They would work together to track down the gang suspected of murder, kidnapping, theft and firearms offences.

Jussi yawned.

That night, he was waiting at the small airport in Kemi to take a commercial flight to Gothenburg. He had completed some swift airport shopping for a change of clothes and some essentials. Now, he sat with a hamburger and diet soda, which he enjoyed much more than expected. He didn't eat fast food as a rule, but his eating habits had been so erratic over the past 24 hours that he now classified this as a good meal; he wolfed it down gratefully.

There was a lot on Jussi's mind. He had been pleased to receive the news that there had been four travellers: two men and two women, on the flight to Gothenburg, which he took to signify that Heli was alive and well. Of course, the passport information from the flight was fictitious as it referred to people that didn't exist on any database. However, even if they had missed the gang in Finland, they knew which city they were probably in.

After stretching his legs for a few minutes, the flight was called, and he smiled at the flight attendant as he stowed his bag and made himself comfortable. The trip took about three hours in total and involved a short stop in Stockholm.

He almost immediately fell asleep on the first flight, only waking up on arrival in Stockholm - he had really needed the rest. Now he felt ready for anything. He had a short wait until his next flight, so he spent it walking around the large terminal to stretch his legs, browsing among the electronic equipment. He bought a large takeaway cup of his favourite coffee with an extra shot for good measure.

The next flight was called, which turned out to be another short one.

He walked off the plane, ready to meet his Swedish colleagues and begin the search. This time nobody was waiting at the airport. Checking his messages, he noted a text message stating they would meet him at the central police station.

"Oh, that's just great!" Jussi mumbled to himself under his breath.

He thought there wasn't time to meet at the station and just wanted to get on with it. Perhaps, the local police could do all the desktop research and locate potential hotels? He could then focus on possible suspects, such as four people checking into a hotel or maybe two couples?

Jussi was by nature an action-oriented person and now desperate to find Heli. What were his choices, though? He didn't know Gothenburg well enough and would need a considerable amount of help. However, he was concerned that the local force would not be as keen as him to find Heli, as they didn't know her. He also didn't relish going through the whole story again, but he would just have to grit his teeth and bear it.

Jussi took a taxi to the police station and prepared for the task ahead.

PAYMENT DUE

Sabrina spent considerable time preparing for the meeting with the buyer. She usually travelled light through experience but always seemed to have just the right outfit, jewellery and cosmetics to look amazing. Oleg and Stanislav had discussed it several times and couldn't understand how she always managed to look so good. The truth was that she was a master of the capsule wardrobe, and she could wear her clothes and accessories in different combinations. A simple black skirt could be dressed up with a gold top, or down, with a white blouse. Many of her clothes were also relatively small, as she was fond of using her appearance to get what she wanted. Sabrina usually had a plan and, more often than not, she succeeded.

When Sabrina was finally ready, she went to the hotel lobby, where Stanislav and Oleg were waiting. They had decided that four people together was something best avoided. Therefore, Heli remained in her room, nervously awaiting news.

The men had their newly purchased weapons concealed and loaded. They also wore equal expressions of anticipation and gravity. Oleg and Stanislav saw the end result of great wealth clearly in their minds. They had no intention of letting anyone interrupt their long-awaited payday. If the buyer and Sabrina agreed on the price, they would be wealthy enough to go wherever and do whatever they wanted.

The group left the hotel and walked the ten-minute route to another more prominent hotel. Sabrina had insisted on them staying at a different place to separate them from the meeting itself.

It was dark and becoming cold, so Sabrina buttoned her coat and began to think about the size of the drink she would have after the end of the forthcoming discussion. She walked up the steps of the large hotel on the square. She thought it was a newer one as she didn't recognise it from a previous visit. The hotel was modern in design, with pink and blue lights highlighting stark modern metal and stone sculptures.

Sabrina walked through the foyer and took in her surroundings, approaching the brushed metal reception desk with its concrete facade. She was due to meet the buyer in one of the meeting rooms. As it was not immediately apparent where that was, she enquired as to its whereabouts.

The receptionist was dressed all in black, and her face was fixed with a permanent smile, accentuated with bright red lipstick. She introduced herself as Maria and asked if she could help in any way.

Sabrina announced her purpose and was directed down a flight of stairs towards the conference suite. She followed the directions: down two flights of concrete steps, past striking modern art on the walls and finally through a glass door at the bottom.

Through the door was a refreshment area with several meeting rooms lined up on the right. The last meeting room was labelled 'Overton', the contact's name that she had been requested to meet. She took a deep breath and smiled to overcome her nerves, uncharacteristically showing at that moment, and tapped on the door.

It was opened by a smart young man, wearing a narrow, perfectly-fitted dark grey suit, purple tie and matching pocket handkerchief. He smiled at her arrival and invited her in. She followed him into the room.

Inside was an equally well-dressed elderly man with silver grey hair, dressed in a dark blue suit. He was sitting at the boardroom-style table, with a coffee set, mineral water and sandwiches, set to one side.

"Welcome Sabrina!" the elderly man bellowed enthusiastically. "I've been waiting for you for some time. I arrived here early as I was so excited about your discovery."

"It's very nice to meet you err...Mr. Overton?"

"Oh, it's not Overton, of course, but you can call me Eric, that should serve our purposes for this conversation. Please take a seat."

The younger man, who Sabrina took to be an Assistant of some kind, withdrew her chair and deftly replaced it as she sat down.

"Right, that's nicer. Would you like a cup of coffee or tea?"

"That would be nice. Black coffee, thank you."

The character in front of her had taken her by surprise. She hadn't been expecting to see this polite gentleman.

He must be a private collector, she told herself.

Eric poured her a coffee, and they settled into their chairs for the negotiation. Eric nodded to the young man who left the room with a respectful nod.

"So, you are interested in our little collection?" Sabrina asked.

"Oh yes, I am, young lady. Especially the egg. You have no idea how long I've been waiting to see one of the missing ones."

"So, the egg is for yourself?"

"Good gracious, no. I'm merely a retained consultant. The

prospective buyer is someone you will never meet. However, I've been instructed to make a handsome offer if the collection is as genuine and as interesting as you have described it."

Sabrina smiled and removed each item carefully from her bag, unrolling each one and placing them carefully on the table in front of him.

"May I?" Eric enquired and gestured to pick up one of the objects.

"Of course, please do," she answered.

Eric placed a jeweller's eyeglass onto one eye and inspected the items one by one. He muttered to himself as he did so. When he got to the egg, he spent a good ten minutes examining every part of it. He removed a small kit and dabbed some solution onto the egg, adding it to another solution. He scraped gently at one part and looked at the scraper intently, placing it onto a digital device. After a few final moments of consideration, Eric let out a long sigh, and a smile gradually crept across his face.

"Well, I have some news for you, Sabrina."

"Yes?" she asked expectantly.

"The collection you have brought me is quite perfect and completely genuine - and the egg? Well, that really is something special and is indeed a beauty to behold. Please tell me the story of how you acquired this."

"I can tell you some of it."

She spent a few minutes recounting the story of the underground hiding place. She left out the assorted crimes committed to reach that point.

"Well, there's no doubt that it's genuine, and the story you tell, although quite incredible, would be a reasonable reason for these valuables turning up in Finland. Someone either hid them there to protect them or stole them and wanted to use them later. And you have found them through an exciting treasure hunt. Well, well, well."

"Now that you've inspected them, are you interested in making an offer?" Sabrina asked.

"Oh yes, of course. As I said, I'm already authorised to make a single offer, no more, no less. Would you like to know what that is?"

"That's why I'm here," smiled Sabrina.

"In that case, as you have more items here than expected, I have an offer of thirty million US dollars on the table for you. As I said, there is no negotiation available. I think you'll find that you won't get a better offer anywhere else. Especially within the small field of interest that would want to keep such a transaction - confidential."

"That's a serious offer. However, we were hoping for a little more." Sabrina replied, trying her luck.

"It's up to you, Sabrina. Others may want what you have, but not everyone is as honest as I am. I can tell you that if you say no to this offer, your life may become more complicated than you could ever expect. Take the offer. Take it now. - please."

Sabrina thought for a moment. She had been offered more than initially quoted and could imagine that dealing with other buyers could be risky and complicated. The gang also needed to get away as soon as possible.

"Very well," Sabrina replied. "I will accept your offer on behalf of the others, provided we can arrange a swift payment. How and when will the money be paid?"

"Oh, that's quite simple. I can have the money wired to a bank account of your choice right away. I have my computer with me, and it'll be a matter of just a few minutes to make the transaction. Shall I proceed?"

Sabrina nodded in agreement, and with that, he picked up his phone and called his associate, who entered the room with another man. His assistant sat at the far corner, and the newcomer stood by the door.

"One cannot be too careful these days, you know. I am honest, and I'm sure you are too, but just in case, my associates will take care that everything goes nice and smoothly, with no hitches. I also have more associates inside the hotel."

"Quite right," Sabrina said. "And of course, so do I. Purely for security reasons," she added.

She slid over a paper with the account details for the transfer.

"Then we are evenly matched and have as much mutual trust as is practical, under the circumstances," he smiled. "I will make the transfer now, and we should remain here until you have confirmation that the money has reached your bank. We have plenty of coffee here to keep us going, and there are also some sandwiches if you wish. Now, please excuse me for a few minutes. This is a calculation for which I need full concentration."

Eric worked silently on his laptop and confirmed that the transaction had gone through successfully after a few minutes.

"And now, please wait for a short while and call your bank for confirmation. When you have received this, our business together is concluded."

They drank coffee silently, and after a few minutes, Sabrina began to pace the room while calling her bank. She was relieved to find that the wire transfer had been almost instantaneous, and the bank confirmed they had received the funds.

Outside, Oleg and Stanislav were becoming nervous. After a brief discussion, Oleg remained outside to watch the hotel's front. At the same time, Stanislav casually walked in and ordered a coffee from the lounge, taking a seat in the lobby.

Back in the meeting room, things had gone remarkably smoothly. Sabrina watched while one of Eric's associates wrapped up the valuables once more and packed them into a carry-on style black-wheeled bag that he retrieved from under the table. Eric and Sabrina shook hands, and she watched the treasure walk out of the door.

Sabrina called the bank again, just to be sure, and they confirmed once again that the money was in the account. She asked for an email confirmation and sat down for a few more minutes to await its receipt.

It was with great relief that she opened the PDF attached to the email and read its contents. Each of her partners-in-crime would be entitled to ten per cent of the proceeds, which they currently thought, would total twenty million dollars. She had already calculated it would result in two million dollars each and, therefore, six million dollars in total for the three of her partners. After paying half of the total proceeds, ten million, to their elusive partner, she would be left with four million for herself.

If she told them the price was thirty million, they would want more. This way, if she told them the proceeds were twenty million, she could still give them and her secret partner their shares and have fourteen million left for herself. She decided this was a much more satisfactory result.

When she was ready, she walked up the stairs to the lobby. She smiled at Stanislav, whom she noted was now waiting in the chair, casually watching her over a newspaper. The area was now almost empty, so he moved towards her and asked if everything was fine, at which she nodded it was.

They walked out of the hotel together, and Oleg, standing across the street, watched them cross the road and walk towards their own hotel. Oleg followed a respectful distance behind, monitoring for possible threats until they were safely back. After a few minutes, he decided everything was okay and followed them inside.

They walked straight up to Sabrina's room, and she opened the door. Heli was sitting eagerly in a chair at the other side of the room, waiting intently for news. When they were all back in the room, and the information had been shared - they ordered champagne.

They ordered two bottles of Dom Perignon vintage, the most expensive on the hotel menu to celebrate. They opened the bottles on arrival and chinked their glasses together. They had just made millions; Sabrina had even more reason to be happy. They proceeded to sit down and discuss the deal that had been agreed upon.

Sabrina confirmed she had received a transfer of twenty million dollars that would be split in the pre-agreed fashion. She would take care of those further transfers shortly. Nobody questioned it could have been any different; in fact, they had been a little apprehensive that Sabrina may have to accept less. None of them had expected the deal to go so smoothly. Their most significant concern had been a possible double-cross by the buyer. Oleg had been ready to act if this had been the case, but no, it had been a smooth business transaction.

The chink of their glasses and the first drink of chilled champagne felt good to one and all. They proceeded to discuss their various exit routes for the following day.

They had all decided to leave the country by sea; by now, this seemed the safest route. Two of them would take separate ferries to Germany. At the same time, the other two would head for Denmark, again on two different ferries. The level of security on ferries was more relaxed, and they decided there was less chance of discovery.

The money was to be distributed that night. For this purpose, they had all pre-equipped themselves with a selection of overseas bank accounts, with locations ranging from Bahrain to Belize. They supplied Sabrina with the details, and she quietly sat on the bed to transfer the money while the others continued to drink champagne. She also sent a message and a transfer to their silent partner and moved her millions into her own chosen banks. When the task was completed, she asked the others to check their accounts.

After a short while, Heli confirmed safe receipt of her transfer. She was delighted and poured another glass of champagne. Due to the late hour and country time differences of their chosen banks, Neither Oleg nor Stanislav could confirm their transfers but were confident everything would go smoothly as arranged. They would check tomorrow.

Later that evening, the gang sat in Sabrina's and Heli's hotel room, sharing their latest plans.

Sabrina explained that she would head to Thailand. Firstly, she would fly to Bangkok and then travel onwards to Phuket, where a luxury hotel room awaited her for as long as she wanted. She planned to relax and work on her suntan.

Heli announced that she would travel to the Caribbean and 'get lost' somewhere in the islands. With her dream of a beachside home in sight, she would land in Saint Lucia and island-hop until she found the right one to remain on. She didn't plan to return to Finland or even Europe ever again.

Stanislav planned to travel around South America and just keep moving. He thought it seemed like an excellent place to get lost, and he planned to start in Belize and stay in low-key establishments, avoiding the big cities where possible. He'd been in similar situations before and wanted to stay under the radar as much as he could.

As for Oleg, in the end, he had decided to return to Russia. He had some interests there that he planned to expand. He didn't dream of a Caribbean beach but instead of a business empire and the opportunity to be an important man. Plenty of female company, a luxury car and a bodyguard were just some of the accessories he was looking forward to.

◆ ◆ ◆

Jussi finished his meeting with the Swedish police that had gone smoother than expected. He walked out of the room with his new detective colleagues and a list of possible hotels to check. However, the list was long.

There were a surprising number of hotels in Gothenburg. The gang may also have travelled further afield, inside the country. Not outside of the country yet, though, Jussi assumed. They probably still had their kidnap victim with them, and the risk would be too significant. In the absence of any other leads, the only possible way of finding them would be some good old-fashioned police work.

Between their small team and the general alert that was being circulated, they still had a chance of finding the gang within the next 24 hours. More than that, Jussi was very concerned for Heli's safety as they hadn't been contacted with any demands. Considering the gang's history, there was even a possibility of her lying dead somewhere.

Jussi let his colleagues do the talking in Swedish as they travelled around the hotels. Max did the driving while Kris accompanied him and did the introductions. Jussi spoke some Swedish, so he could understand most of the conversations and ask occasional questions in Swedish, or English if his memory failed him. Both Max and Kris were quite determined, and Jussi warmed to their personalities quickly. They had understood the urgency from his perspective, and there were no complaints about the sudden extension of their shifts. If suitably fueled with coffee and cinnamon buns, there was a distinct possibility of them outlasting Jussi in terms of energy. He was feeling the effects of the last few days, and the short nap on the plane hadn't made up for his recent frantic activities.

At 1.10 am, Jussi turned to his new colleagues.

"Thank you for your help, but as we haven't had any success with this approach so far, let's go and get some sleep. After a few hours rest and a good breakfast, we can start fresh in the morning."

No one protested, and they all agreed to meet at 8 am to start the search with renewed energy.

Heli awoke in the morning to find Sabrina packing.

"Time to go sleepy head, we have money to spend," she smiled.

Heli went to the bathroom and by the time she returned, Sabrina was ready and waiting by the door.

"I'm leaving now Heli. It's time to go."

"Okay! Well, good luck Sabrina! It's been an interesting experience. Take care, I'll miss you."

"Me too," Sabrina said, giving Heli an affectionate hug.

"Look after yourself, Heli, and please don't trust anyone from now on. Go and find your beach."

"You too. Enjoy Thailand!" and with that, she was gone.

Sabrina was the only one in the group who had lied about her plans. Even though she was leaving on a ferry, her final destination was not Thailand. She would continue onwards to Singapore so that even if one of the others were caught and did a deal with the police, she would not be found in Thailand. Sabrina always planned ahead.

She also sent a simple text to Oleg and Stanislav.

Time to go! it said.

On her way out of the hotel, she took the memory card out of her phone, snapped it in two and threw her phone in the rubbish bin for good measure.

Sabrina was gone for good.

Heli sat on the bed. She had been taken aback by the hug from Sabrina; she would indeed miss her. She had been the one whom Heli had trusted, and she had followed her guidance on several occasions.

Heli sighed and stood up.

She had some time to wait for the ferry, but Sabrina leaving early had unnerved her a little. She decided to go now as well, and packed quickly, planning to go shopping in the city for a new wardrobe before leaving on her own journey.

When she was ready, she went downstairs to get a coffee and met Oleg and Stanislav at breakfast. She hastily drank a cup of coffee with them and said her farewells. She was happy to distance herself from these two, whom she quite simply saw as hired killers and didn't want to be around them without Sabrina.

Sabrina always seemed so confident and self-assured, with the ability to get out of trouble. She had felt safe with her, even with the two thugs.

Heli set off with her small bag and headed for the station.

Oleg and Stanislav were just finishing their breakfast when Jussi and Kris casually entered the hotel and approached the reception desk. Stanislav spotted Jussi and tagged Oleg by the arm. He motioned him to the coffee-making area, hidden from view from the reception desk by a wall. They lingered there for a moment on the pretext of making drinks.

◆ ◆ ◆

For Jussi and his new colleagues, it was their fourth hotel of the morning, with a further six the night before, and still no success. There had no updates from the officers at the police station either, who were busy checking on credit cards and travel networks. Jussi felt compelled to continue the hotel-by-hotel search because, at least this way, they were doing something. Therefore, he continued the search with Max and Kris, together with some uniformed officers.

The young receptionist couldn't help the detectives, but just as he was about to give up hope, she suddenly said something quite offhand.

"Oh, there were those Russians who paid cash. They said their credit cards had been stolen."

"Are they still here?" Jussi asked expectantly.

"Well, there were two rooms, a lady and a gentleman in each one. Two couples. One room has been checked out already, but the other is still occupied. They are due to check out at noon today."

Jussi checked his watch. The time was now 9.30 am. This was exciting news and meant there was a possibility of one or more of the criminals still being in the hotel.

He motioned to Kris, who called Max, asking him to bring the additional officers as backup.

"If it's them, they could be armed, and they know how to use their weapons," Jussi added, in warning.

At this point, Oleg and Stanislav were observing developments.

One of the uniformed officers positioned himself by the front door; another walked through the lobby to the rear of the building. The detectives made their way upwards, two by the stairs and two by the lift. All exits were being covered.

The two gang members quickly decided that they needed to move now or never, while they still had the advantage of surprise.

"Let's go now!" said Stanislav shaking his friend's hand and looking him in the eye.

Oleg patted him on the back and motioned him to go straight out of the front door. It seemed the best way to take on a single officer if needed, without being spotted by the others.

Stanislav strode out of the breakfast area and straight towards the reception desk. He picked up a newspaper and casually walked towards the door, opening the newspaper.

The police officer held his hand up with which to stop him.

"Stop, police!" he demanded.

The officer didn't stand a chance. Oleg appeared from around the corner, firing round after round at him. The officer hit the floor with a thud. Glass shattered everywhere inside the lobby. The noise was deafening. People were running and screaming, both inside the hotel and on the street.

Now, Oleg and Stanislav were running for the door. They may have thought they'd got away but hadn't planned on another officer outside, who already had her gun drawn. She had a clear shot at Stanislav as he ran out of the door.

The officer fired twice, and Stanislav fell. As he did so, he returned fire. This gave Oleg the space to continue running. Oleg looked back at Stanislav as he did so. They both knew that although they would try and protect each other - if one was lost, the other should go. As Stanislav lay motionless on the pavement, Oleg decided one of them was already lost.

He ran as fast as he could and ducked down a side street, placing his weapon in his small bag as he ran. He gradually reduced his run to a walk and dumped his cap and jacket into a space between walls. Oleg continued to stroll down the street until he found a clothing store, where he calmly walked in and purchased a new green wax jacket.

Moments later, he strode out into the sunshine, went into a café, and ordered a coffee. More police were appearing now and running would be suicidal; he needed to blend, collect his thoughts, and find a place to hide. His training from his past life had kicked in, as he calmly considered his options. At the same time, he was thinking about Stanislav. He had known him for some time and was sorry he had fallen. They had both almost made it.

As soon as Jussi and the other officers heard the shots, they ran downstairs and entered the reception area with guns drawn, straight into the chaos of the lobby.

Other police cars had arrived now, and an officer was on his radio while holding his colleague, who was possibly alive but if so, barely - with multiple gunshot wounds.

"Where did they go?" Jussi demanded of the shaking receptionist, who pointed outside.

On the street, the officer who had shot Stanislav was standing holding a gun over him, simultaneously watching the direction in which Oleg had ran. He gestured in that direction, and Jussi and the other detectives sprinted down the street in pursuit.

Within an hour, a city cordon had been arranged, cameras were being monitored, and a helicopter was in the air. The ports, highways and airports were also on high alert. Everyone was searching for Oleg.

The police are highly effective at locating fugitives but not nearly as effective at searching for someone who had concealed themselves so close to the crime. One of Oleg's specialities was to be able to hide in plain sight.

After yet another costume change, he had made his way quietly into an apartment close by, where he remained, calmly helping himself to the contents of the fridge. Its owner had not yet returned, and it would be all the worse for them if they did. In the meantime, Oleg had found the perfect hiding place.

Heli breathed a long sigh as the train pulled out of the station. She sipped her large latte and snuggled into her seat. The train was quite full, mostly with smartly dressed commuters going to work. Many people were engrossed in their smartphones, tablets or laptops.

She contented herself with reading a novel in English, purchased at a small kiosk: something about racing horses and falling in love ; it passed the time along the journey.

Heli always stayed connected to the outside world. Now, she had deliberately disconnected from technology, thinking it would reduce the possibility of being found. The only thing she currently possessed was her latest prepaid phone that she intended to dump as soon as she could purchase a new one. This would formally end her relationship with the rest of the gang. She wouldn't even have their telephone numbers and would already feel safer. Even if one of them were to be arrested and tell all, she would already be long gone. She also intended to withdraw some cash to pay for her travel where possible, feigning the excuse of losing her credit card.

It was liberating for Heli to plan her new life like this, and it felt surprisingly easy to do. Only lying to and leaving Jussi had been hard. She was sad about using the person for whom she had most feelings and leaving him without knowing what had happened to her. He was an adult, though, and this would pass, she told herself. Everything passes with time, and for her, the money would help.

The train arrived in Malmo. People started to get off, and it seemed those remaining would be staying on the train until Copenhagen. She had travelled this way before and expected security to be light as usual. Unless there were a terrorist threat, passing through should be a formality. She did have a nagging sensation that the border authorities may have been warned of her false passport, but that seemed unlikely.

Her concerns were unfounded, and after half an hour's journey, she arrived safely at Copenhagen airport. She made her way to the ticket booth and purchased a ticket to Saint Lucia. It had crossed her mind to travel first class, but then again, she wanted to draw as little attention to herself as possible and pay cash for her ticket. Travelling economy and spending as little as possible was the best way to do this, she decided. There would be plenty of time for luxuries later.

Inside the airport, she purchased some snacks, water and a couple more novels for the trip. She paid cash for a new prepaid phone and went to the bathroom to get rid of the old one, breaking the sim card and dropping everything into a bin. Her one taste of luxury was to purchase access to a business lounge, paying cash to enter.

Once in, she stretched out and relaxed. She treated herself to a large glass of wine and some snacks while waiting for her flight. She tried to remain calm, although she knew she would be nervous until they had taken off and were in the air, leaving Europe behind.

Sometime later, her flight appeared on the monitors, and she strolled the long walk from one end of the airport to the other. Boarding was smooth, with a light load of passengers and the lucky draw of a row of three seats to herself.

After taking off, she stretched out, and within minutes her eyes closed. It was the best sleep she had enjoyed for some time. Not even the drinks service woke her. In her dreams, she was already safe and living her new life.

Oleg remained in his borrowed apartment for a couple of days. Luckily nobody had arrived at the door. After that, he decided it was safe enough to move. He changed into different clothes and strolled through the city. He was well-practised at melting into the background and was pleased with the cap he had found in the apartment, which helped him to look even more anonymous. He had purchased a new mobile phone on his way and contacted an old friend of his, making arrangements to leave Stockholm and travel onwards to Moscow.

A couple of hours later, he was picked up outside the apartment and taken to another one. There, he spent some time making some changes to his appearance. He coloured his hair and put on glasses; changing his appearance was one of Oleg's particular skills. With this disguise, together with a change of documents, he was ready to move again.

After a couple more hours, the car returned. The driver drove across Finland and onwards through the Russian border, where he caught a train to Moscow.

Oleg had made it - he was back safe in his beloved Russia.

HIDING PLACES

Sabrina exhaled a long and satisfied sigh as she glanced across the swimming pool. She picked up her fresh, ice-cold orange juice that had appeared by her side and listened as the ice cubes gently clinked on the side of the glass.

She took in the spectacular views around her of the impressive city-state of Singapore. Even at nine o'clock in the morning, it was hot, really hot and also humid. Not so sticky yet as to be uncomfortable, especially not in her bikini, but more than enough to know that she was exactly where she wanted to be. She was in an exotic country, with fantastic food, plenty of shopping, and new adventures ahead.

Over the past fortnight, Sabrina had been staying in some of the top hotels in Singapore. Due to the high level of service and duration of stay booked, she was being treated like royalty. She didn't want to stay too long in any one hotel, though. It made her feel more comfortable to be anonymous, although anonymity was not something that came easily to her.

It'd been a straightforward matter to reach Singapore, and she was happy to make this her base for a while. It combined everything she wanted in one place, except beaches, but she could holiday anytime and wherever she wanted now. There were plenty of luxurious resorts with amazing beaches around South East Asia.

Sabrina stretched again and turned over to watch the sky as she lay thinking. She had plenty of time to think now. She was currently considering whether to buy property in Singapore. She would love to do that and have a fantastic apartment overlooking the cityscape, with a lovely pool. However, it was still too early to lay down any roots.

Probably better I stay mobile for now, she thought.

Heli's plane landed at Saint Lucia's Hewonorra airport. It seemed like an age between landing and stepping onto the tarmac, but she was thrilled to do it.

She took a bus for the short transfer towards the small terminal. It was sweltering, but Heli was not concerned and simply removed some of the layers she'd been wearing on the plane.

The process through passport control and immigration was simple, despite some mild concern on Heli's part. She had no suitcase to collect, which also made things more straightforward.

She arrived landside and walked straight across to the tourist information stand. After a few minutes' discussion, she arranged a booking at a hotel across the island, sufficiently remote for her to feel safe and in a holiday mood.

Firstly, it was time to shop. She had arrived with very little in the way of clothes, and although she didn't expect to need much of a wardrobe here, a few things: a couple of summer dresses, swimming costumes, t-shirts and some pairs of shorts, would be essential.

She took a taxi down to a small shopping centre in the town of Castries. There wasn't much choice, but within a couple of hours, with the help of several cold drinks, she had put together a makeshift wardrobe.

I enjoy living like this, Heli thought to herself.

The idea of buying a wardrobe on arrival and then doing the same at the next island, with no baggage in tow, was very attractive indeed.

Later, when she arrived at the hotel, which seemed largely open-air, she was offered a rum cocktail. She was then shown to her suite. After hanging her new clothes, she changed into a swimsuit: a bright emerald green two-piece. She opened the French doors and stepped directly into the pool. She was happy with her choice of room and could easily see herself spending her days swimming between it and the swim-up bar: drinking mojitos and chatting to the smiling, laid-back barman whilst snacking on delicious fried fish.

A fortnight later, Heli had been swimming again, as part of her routine. She smiled to herself as she finished her lunch. She had eaten fresh, crispy prawns with a mango salad - delicious. She licked her lips and picked up her ice-cold glass of white wine. It was hot there - tropical, but an occasional downpour freshened the air. As she sipped her drink, the ice-cold liquid refreshed her throat so well that she soon finished it and ordered another.

Heli had absolutely nothing to do today and was delighted about it. She wasn't sure how long it would take to become bored of this place, but she was pretty happy for now.

In the morning, she had slept long and enjoyed breakfast in bed. After a stroll around the hotel grounds, she sat down for lunch. She had arranged a cocoa body wrap and massage at the spa in the afternoon, and would have a nice siesta afterwards.

Perhaps tomorrow I'll book another sightseeing trip and also get started in the gym, she thought.

There were a few other guests in the hotel, but Heli kept herself to herself. She kept a novel with her, which, together with dark sunglasses, allowed her to maintain distance from any interested parties. She had no wish to converse about anything except occasional small talk and, if asked directly, would say that she was taking an extended vacation after a busy time at work.

She hardly thought about the previous weeks' events, and if she did, it was about Jussi. In her mind, she had tried to file him away into her past to forget him. Anyway, today, her mind was blank as she stretched out on the sunbed of her terrace once more.

Oleg grunted as he looked out of the window into the street. It was a cold, dark rainy morning in Sergiyev Posad. He had decided to stay in a smaller place for a while, convenient for Moscow but a reasonable distance away.

He had rented a small apartment for cash from a rental agency - something non-descript. This would allow him to lie low for a month, then moving on to another small town in the area.

Oleg was always on his guard, especially after the incident in Finland. He was also painfully aware that Stanislav was dead, shot by the police while trying to escape. He knew how easily this could happen if a situation erupted, faced with no choice but to fight or run. However, it was playing on his mind.

He had chosen a pleasant town with a few places to eat: good Russian food with good Russian vodka. He'd never been a man to run to expensive tastes, at least not until now. He had been known to choose excellent wine, but he usually just preferred the company of his favourite things. He was not a cook, and he ate out almost every night, varying the place each time so as not to become memorable. He didn't want to be concerned about people discussing his business with him. Although, he had a way of dissuading people from engaging him in conversation if he wanted to.

He took another glug of strong coffee and sat down to check his new phone for news. He'd been the only one in the gang to have been following the case closely and was satisfied that the world had forgotten them after only two weeks. Oleg smiled to himself as he considered the future. Life was about to change. The time would come when he would buy that new black hummer and superior apartment in Moscow. He lit another cigarette and relaxed into his chair.

Jussi looked out of his hotel room in Gothenberg and surveyed the weather. It was raining - actually sleeting. Although the day had been sunny, it had turned cold again.

He threw on his coat and left the room to get some fresh air and clear his head. He was hungry. It had been another long day, and he was beginning to tire of these. He'd been working with his Swedish colleagues, participating in virtual meetings with Interpol representatives around Europe. The group had been trying to follow a trail of breadcrumbs that would take them to where the gang had disappeared, which was easier said than done.

It had been a stroke of pure chance to walk into the hotel where the suspects had been staying. However, since then, the rest of them seemed to have gone to ground, and the dead man wasn't going to give anything away. His papers had been false, and he had only cash and a few clothes in his possession. Neither credit cards nor mobile phones had been found. The body of Stanislav now rested in the morgue.

That morning, Jussi received some news about Heli. The information had shocked him. On the hotel's CCTV system, she had been identified leaving the hotel alone, seemingly of her own free will. She had also been spotted on various video feeds in the city, apparently shopping.

For various reasons, thoughts that she had been involved with the gang had entered his mind from time to time, but he had dismissed them as ridiculous. After all, how could she have so convincingly lied to him throughout their time together in Helsinki and Rauma? However, it was now becoming clear that she had been part of the gang.

From what stage, though?

He wasn't sure, but rather than being an innocent kidnap victim, it seemed she was a fugitive from justice. The revelation had made him feel sick at first, and it was hard even to think about it, but he was now sure. Anyway, whatever the case, she too had disappeared.

Jussi's role in Sweden was to work with the investigating team for as long as was useful. However, he could already see that his work here was nearing it's end; he was also looking forward to going home to Rauma.

He left the hotel and shrank into his coat as the cold wind gripped him. With no particular plans, he wandered around the old streets. He could've been enjoying the architecture had it not been for the weather. He quickened his pace and came across a small Thai restaurant on a street corner.

Thai food - perfect. Just what I need right now, Jussi decided.

A smiling young waitress greeted him, and he took a seat at a small table by the bar. After ordering some Pad Thai and red wine, she brought the bottle over and poured him a large glass. He took a drink, and the warmth of the wine and delicious smells of the restaurant brought him back to life.

Jussi's phone suddenly rang loudly, and he fumbled for it, aware of the disapproving looks from the diners seated close by. He answered and heard a familiar voice at the other end.

"Jussi? Is that you?"

"Heli? What the? Where are you? Are you okay?"

"I'm fine, Jussi, and I'm safe."

With his mind whirling, he asked:

"Were you part of the gang? Have you been involved in this the whole time? Did you lie to me about everything? Do you know how much trouble you are in?"

"I just want to tell you something: I didn't hurt anyone, and I had no control over the situation I was in."

Jussi strode out of the restaurant onto the street.

"Heli, you are being sought for suspected murder, do you realise that?"

"Yes, I know. I just wanted you to know those things were not my fault. I didn't want you to think bad of me."

"What do you expect? You lied to me, Heli. You've committed serious crimes! Where are you now? You need to turn yourself in, and I will do my best to help you, but you must tell me everything."

"Merry Christmas, Jussi. Take care."

With that, Heli rang off.

Jussi stared at his phone for a few moments in shock. Then he checked the number to return the call; it had been withheld.

He re-entered the restaurant just as his food arrived. Jussi's mind was racing. At least she was okay and may not have been directly involved in the murders, but she was still an accessory. She had cared enough to call him but had given no clue as to where she was.

Jussi began to pick at his food and took a large gulp of the wine. Somehow, it didn't taste quite as good as it had a few moments ago. He tried to eat some of the food, finished the wine and left for his hotel.

◆ ◆ ◆

The following day, Jussi booked a flight to Helsinki.

He left at midday, after working at the desk in his hotel room for the morning. The journey was quicker this time, with a direct flight.

After the trip, he drove back home to Rauma.

He walked into his apartment that evening, unpacked, ate and went to bed. After a short time on his tablet computer, while trying to dismiss thoughts of Heli from his mind, he realised it was Christmas Eve the following day; December had flown by. This wasn't the way he wanted to feel when approaching his favourite holiday.

Jussi turned over and went to sleep.

It was Christmas Eve, and snow was falling outside.

Despite the festive atmosphere, Jussi had been in no mood to take any time off work, and for the first time, volunteered to work over Christmas. He had received a couple of invitations from well-meaning friends but couldn't face trying to celebrate with anyone.

Better to focus on work, he had decided.

The police station was quiet, with just a skeleton staff operating the desk, phones and emergency response service. Christmas Eve morning found him sitting at his own desk, nursing a large cup of coffee and surfing the internet. He was tracing Heli's route across and out of the Nordic countries, as much as he knew or could guess. He yawned and swept his mouse around different places to where she could have travelled.

She could be anywhere, he thought to himself. *Perhaps somewhere in Africa or India? Anywhere in Asia? Or South America, maybe?*

He tired of this activity after a while, clicked his mouse, and the screen disappeared. He stood up and walked to the window overlooking the street. There was no doubt about it. No matter what Heli had done, he was missing her terribly, but was angry at the same time. He couldn't dismiss her from his mind and had considered different ways of how to do this. None of them had worked so far.

It was a long day, that day. He left the station late that evening, walked through the old town and finally down his favourite street: Kuninkaankatu.

The winter scene was spectacular. The enormous tree on the square was lit, and festive lights and decorations adorned the street and sparkled in windows. Large flakes of snow were falling and gently settling on him. He could imagine people enjoying their Christmas Eve Dinner: drinking, eating and having fun.

Jussi put his head down determinedly and strode on until he reached his apartment, glancing at the museum on the square as he did so, where the story had begun.

Once inside his home, he opened a bottle of wine and heated a ready meal in the microwave. He raised his glass to Heli as he toasted out loud:

"Merry Christmas, Heli - wherever you are!"

UNWELCOME VISITORS

Christmas came and went in Singapore. Sabrina enjoyed celebrating the new year. However, she was starting to tire of being in the same place. Not that Singapore wasn't a perfect location for her in every way, but just that she grew tired of things quickly. She had already started to survey the map and consider other locations to where she could travel. However, Sabrina was aware that she didn't want to be identified at the border. So, for the moment, she would have to remain where she was.

That morning, as usual, she was sitting by the pool with her breakfast when she noticed someone walking directly towards her. The man was dressed in a suit and tie.

A little overdressed for this climate, she thought.

The figure continued to walk in her direction and, to her surprise, arrived at her table. The man stopped and addressed her.

"May I join you, Sabrina?"

She was surprised but remained calm and collected. She nodded while trying to work out where he could be from. Anyone that knew her here was a risk.

The man took a seat, leaned back and spoke.

"It seems that you owe me something, Sabrina."

She looked at him with a puzzled expression.

"Who are you?"

"Don't you recognise your business partner?" the man asked.

Sabrina sat upright a little.

"You're Duncan?"

"Well, not exactly, but in my business, it's sometimes necessary to employ an alternative name. Wouldn't you agree?"

"Well, well, this is a nice surprise. Perhaps you need to thank me for a job well done?" said Sabrina, smiling now.

"Sabrina, I virtually gave you this on a plate. You did succeed in finding the treasure, but you left a big mess behind you, didn't you?" he asked accusatively.

"That was just unlucky."

"Unlucky for Stanislav - yes."

"So why are you here? Or do you just like warm climates?"

"Not exactly. I prefer somewhere a little cooler actually."

Sabrina could tell this by his clothing and pallid complexion. She began to feel uncomfortable as he sat considering her for a few moments.

"So, what brings you to Singapore?" she asked again, slightly nervously, to break the silence.

At that moment, the waitress appeared at their table. The man ordered tea and ice water. Sabrina hadn't touched her breakfast but now took a long drink of her iced coffee. When the waitress had retreated out of earshot, the man named Duncan, brought up the original subject.

"I think you owe me something, Sabrina? Did you think I

wouldn't find out about the money? I have connections in all kinds of places, and antiquities is a particular interest of mine. When I was offered a rather rare item, which I recognised, I decided to meet the seller, and I was surprised to learn how much he had paid for it."

"Why would he tell you that? He must have been lying." Sabrina answered, with a slight edge to her tone.

She was already thinking about how she could escape from this situation.

Duncan answered, "People tend to be quite talkative in my company. Oh, I didn't have to do anything nasty Sabrina, we simple became partners, so to speak."

Sabrina looked at him, knowing what was to follow.

"Quite simply, I require the additional ten million dollars that you failed to tell me about."

Sabrina didn't think it was worth denying it now.

"Well, you cannot blame a girl for trying."

She smiled coyly at him, leaning forward and looking into his eyes. He continued to fix her with his stare - unimpressed.

"This is simple, Sabrina. We'll go back to your room, and you will transfer the funds to me, along with your total share from this venture. I'm not a violent man. I am a businessman. I could have you killed, but I'm much more interested in the money. I will even leave you something to play with here in Singapore for a while. After all, you did find what I wanted, but now I want my money, plus interest for your dishonesty and my inconvenience."

"How did you know about the egg in the first place?"

Sabrina took the opportunity to change the subject and ask a question she'd been dying to know for some time.

"My ancestor was involved in keeping it safe over the years. The story eventually passed down through my family until I heard about it. Unfortunately, the previous caretaker had not been entirely trusting and had hidden the valuables in another place. Therefore, I had to take matters into my own hands and formulate a plan to recover them. At least I was able to recover the information about the paintings before he died."

Sabrina flinched a little.

"As I said, I'm not a bad man Sabrina. That was just a conversation on his death bed. Shall we go now? Or do you wish to finish your breakfast?"

"Maybe I've lost my appetite."

"So be it, Sabrina."

They rose and walked together towards the main hotel building. Sabrina noted another man joining them, who had been waiting behind the glass door.

She was thinking fast as they walked towards the elevator in the large lobby. The man pressed the button, and the lift arrived almost immediately.

Too quick, she thought.

She was desperately trying to think of a plan. It was unlikely she would be able to flee. She would have to rely on her guile to escape the predicament.

Arriving at her floor, the lift opened, and they walked to her room. She opened the door, and the three of them trooped in. Sabrina turned and faced them down.

"Now what?" she asked.

"Now, you will transfer the money from your account to

mine. We will wait here until my bank has confirmed the transaction. Then, we will leave. You may keep $100,000 to play with - call it my parting gift. If I see you again? Well, let's just say it would be a good idea for you to disappear."

Sabrina couldn't argue and reluctantly retrieved her laptop from its case, proceeding to open it. She logged into her account and began setting up the transfer, leaving $100,000 in place.

What happened next was utterly unexpected.

The door flew open with a crash. The other man fell to the floor as a silenced pistol fired two bullets into him with soft thuds. The same happened with Duncan. He keeled over and fell into the glass coffee table, which smashed loudly.

Sabrina sat frozen, looking incredulously at Oleg as he redirected his eyes to her.

"Time to leave," he instructed.

"How did you know?"

"I've been checking on you since you left. I asked a friend of mine to keep an eye on you. When he found you were being traced, it seemed too clever for the police, so I decided to come and help."

Sabrina smiled weakly.

"Well, you got here just in time. This guy was about to steal all my money."

"Perhaps he was annoyed you had stolen from him?"

Oleg smiled back.

"Yes, I guessed. I think I know you now, Sabrina. Don't worry. I'm not desperate for a larger share. Besides, you have more expensive tastes. Come on, let's go!"

It only took two minutes, and they had grabbed some essentials and left the room.

Within another five, they were in a taxi heading away from the hotel.

◆ ◆ ◆

Back in Rauma. Jussi was working at his desk, ploughing through the latest travel information. He had now been seconded to an official task force involving Finland, Sweden, Denmark and other countries within Interpol. They had discovered the trail within Sweden and Denmark but hadn't been able to trace any gang members beyond that.

After two hours of research, Jussi rose from his desk and walked over to the coffee machine, pouring himself a large cupful from the pot. His phone rang, and he put his cup down for a moment as he answered it while looking out of the window. He was surprised by what he heard next.

The caller was a police officer from Singapore, calling about a shooting incident in a hotel room in the city.

Singapore cooperated with Interpol, and according to facial recognition cameras, Sabrina had shown up there - alive and well. They discussed the matter and concluded that although the police there would circulate her photograph, it was unlikely she would remain there for long. Jussi decided to update the rest of the team.

In reality, the two fugitives in Singapore had decided to do precisely the opposite. Oleg was aware that the city was small, and although they could reach a border or airport quickly enough, there was a high risk of them being identified with so much security. Therefore, he had, as usual, already made some arrangements, and had secured a cheap rental apartment for cash in case he required it.

Driving away from the city centre, he asked the driver for them to be dropped off a few blocks from it, and they walked the rest of the way.

After a restless night's sleep, Jussi received a call on his mobile. He was to drive to Helsinki and take a flight direct to Singapore. The Singaporean police were convinced that the couple had not yet left the country and requested the support of the Finnish police. Jussi was excited to go to such a place and have the opportunity to corner his prey. His role would be to work with the local police as a consultant to bring the gang to justice.

He packed quickly after checking what the climate was like in Singapore. He decided smart, lightweight clothes were in order, although he decided to buy some clothes there if he was to stay for a more extended period; he didn't possess many clothes for such weather.

After checking the flight time, he found there was no rush and worked at home for a while. Then he left his apartment to drive to Helsinki.

The journey by road passed quickly, although he still needed to wait for some hours at the airport as the flight didn't depart until midnight.

On arrival at the terminal, he was pleased to have a good meal and a beer before the flight; plane food was not his favourite thing.

In Saint Lucia, after the call to Jussi in Gothenburg, Heli had visited the bar and ordered herself a large rum. She gulped it down as she sank into her usual basket-weave chair. She knew it had been a risk to call Jussi, but it was the result of several sleepless nights thinking about what he might have thought of her.

Heli felt better in one way but worse in another. She realised how much she missed him, and in her imagination, toyed with the idea of him leaving Finland and coming to live with her in Cuba.

We could buy a plantation and grow cocoa beans, spending our weekends on the beach, she mused.

Then she dismissed the idea as stupid. He was a police officer and she was a fugitive from justice, facing serious charges.

On the positive side, she loved the carribean, so here she would stay. There were many benefits to living here, and with independent means, she was in no doubt that she would have a good life. She had no intention of leaving and resigned not to call him again. She finished her drink and wandered over to an empty table.

"Champagne, please," she asked the waiter as he set the menu down in front of her.

Heli dined well that evening on fresh lobster and fresh fruit. By the time she had finished her dinner, the rain had started. Within two minutes, it became heavy tropical rain. She could always tell when it would arrive as she would see the clouds appear across the bay, and then thirty minutes later, the air would turn cool, and the first raindrops would begin - the downpour was then just a couple of minutes away.

Occasionally, Heli would walk into the rain and be surprised at how cold it was. Then, she would quickly go to her room and turn on the taps of the large hot jacuzzi bath by the window. She would sink into the foam with a glass of cold wine from the minibar or champagne if she had remembered to order it.

Tonight, she watched the rain from the terrace as it hammered down like bullets. As she did so, she became aware of a man watching her from the same basket chair, which she, herself, had been sitting in just a short while ago. The man was tanned and attractive, smiling at her with a measured gaze. Sabrina smiled back. The thought of someone else in her jacuzzi that evening was an inviting prospect. However, she had had already made one mistake calling Jussi. She should not risk any possible entanglements here, at least not yet.

Heli left the table and forced herself to ignore the man's gaze as she turned to walk back to her room.

After their phone conversation, Jussi was confused about what exactly she had been involved in? If Heli had been able to read minds, she would have read Jussi's and learned that he had spent some considerable time thinking about her on his flight to Singapore. He hadn't slept during the flight and had sat nursing a cognac in his hand while his mind played through various possible scenarios of Heli's criminal involvement. He didn't want to think about her being involved in anything serious.

How and why had she joined the gang in the first place? Why had she fled the country and gone from being a friend to an international criminal?

It just didn't add up. If she were caught now, she would probably spend the rest of her life in prison. Jussi's only hope was that if her involvement was minor and if she cooperated with the authorities, there might be a way for her to be excluded from serious charges. He wasn't sure, though, and as he had no idea where she was, it seemed an unlikely prospect.

"Would you like anything else?"

His thoughts were interrupted by the Flight Attendant's offer. He thought for a moment but declined. Ordinarily, he would have been quite happy to have a couple of drinks to lull him into relaxation, but he didn't feel like it this time, so he tried to sleep.

◆ ◆ ◆

Heli awoke the following day with a stretch. She'd left the curtains open, and the sun shone in through the open balcony door.

She got out of bed, slightly confused about how she had left the balcony door open. She looked around, and nothing seemed amiss.

I must have had a rum too many last night, she thought to herself.

She walked straight to the large shower and, after a quick blast of cold water, put on her bikini and walked out of the door onto the terrace. She launched herself directly into the water and started to swim. She swam with her head submerged to clear her head of the fog from the previous night's cocktails.

In moments, she reached the other side of the pool and jumped out of the water onto the edge. She pulled back her hair and surveyed the hotel. A few people were having breakfast, a few were sunbathing, and a young couple were playing around at the other end of the pool. She looked for the man that had been watching her the evening before but didn't see him.

She swam back to her room to enjoy a light breakfast, after which she took a relaxing stroll followed by a workout in the gym. She intended to reward herself with some more relaxing spa treatments that day.

◆ ◆ ◆

In Singapore, Sabrina was pacing the living room of the small apartment. In addition to being small, it was poorly decorated and furnished. Just the kind of place that she knew Oleg would have chosen.

"What do we do now, Oleg?"

"We wait, Sabrina. We wait. Try and relax. I've been in these kinds of situations before, and all we have to do is wait. If we panic or make a move too soon, then we are done for."

"It's alright for you to say, Oleg. You've come from some squalid apartment in Moscow. Do you realise how nice my hotel was? It was perfect."

"And you would've been perfectly dead or perfectly broke if I hadn't got you out of that situation. You're sometimes careless, Sabrina. In our profession, you can't afford to be - unless you want to spend your life either in prison or dead."

Sabrina acknowledged his truth with a nod and sat down.

"Okay, so what do we do after things have quietened down?"

"It's already underway. I've arranged for someone to take us by boat to Batam. It's a tourist boat, and we'll be the tourists. There are plenty more warm places to go that serve cold drinks."

Sabrina eyed him for a moment. He was being very protective and genuinely seemed to care for her. She thought for a moment that he probably didn't have anything else in his life, and this was something he probably enjoyed. She smiled at him and sat back, looking at the ceiling. Oleg returned her smile. He was enjoying the continued challenge of being on the run, especially with Sabrina. Perhaps, given time, she would grow closer to him. He shook his head. For the moment, he was happy only to protect her.

The flight to Singapore landed early in the morning, and

with light luggage, Jussi walked straight through security and flashed his passport. He was met by a uniformed police officer, holding a sign with his name on it. They introduced themselves and walked to a car standing at the entrance with the engine running.

The car drove away and went straight to a hotel, where Jussi was asked to be ready in one and a half hours. They would wait for him while he freshened up and ate. He was pleased to have a short break to prepare for the day.

While Jussi was showering at one end of the city, Sabrina was making another uncharacteristic mistake at the other end of it. She had booted up her computer and was checking her main bank account. She had already moved money into different places. However, much of the money remained in her central bank. She smiled to herself as she saw the large amount safely inside. She spent time transferring the funds, in small quantities to not raise suspicion, into other accounts. The incident at the hotel had shaken her, and she didn't want to be in that situation again.

After this task was complete, she checked the map and located the place Oleg had mentioned. What she didn't realise was that her IP address was already being tracked. She had inadvertently left a record of the times she had used the hotel network on their private server, and although this hadn't been a problem then; it was now.

The police had been busy at work, checking different devices, frequency of use and website visits. They were currently tracing and narrowing the search for her down to a few possible locations. Her current address of downtown Sengkang, Singapore, was one of those that appeared on the list.

No sooner had Jussi reached the police station when a senior officer met him with a short bow.

"My name is Inspector Wen Low Han. It seems that you are just in time. We've just found a possible suspect. Shall we go?"

Jussi's mind was firmly back on the hunt. Any cloudiness from the flight immediately disappeared as adrenalin kicked in. He was full of questions as they trotted downstairs to three waiting cars. With lights flashing, they were gone - no sirens were used so as not to alert their targets. They reached the specified location in twenty minutes, and leaving the cars, approached the building.

Some officers spread out and positioned themselves strategically around the area while Jussi and the others arrived at the front door. Ringing the bell of one of the ground floor apartments, they announced their arrival, and after questioning the resident, asked him to open up. It was an elderly gentleman who opened the door with some trepidation. An officer muttered something in Chinese to him, and he opened the door and returned to his apartment with some of the officers. At the same time, others covered the lift, the opposite dwelling and the stairwell.

More police had now arrived outside, and their presence was attracting attention. Although Sabrina's computer had been located there, the network was for the whole building. The police would need to begin checking apartment by apartment. There were four residences in the building: one down, three more to go.

Oleg stood watching the events play out from the apartment above through a small gap in the curtain. He already had an escape plan worked out.

"Sabrina, we have to move," he announced.

Sabrina looked up from her chair, where she'd been watching television, having found a Russian channel of interest.

"Now!" demanded Oleg. "Get your computer and anything else you need, quickly."

Sabrina complied, and within seconds, she was ready to move. She had now put her trust in Oleg, and their roles had reversed.

Oleg explained quickly.

"The area is covered in police. There's a roof exit via a balcony, and from there, we can walk to the next building and down one of the fire escapes, ready?"

"Yes." Sabrina nodded obediently.

She followed Oleg as they made their way to the balcony door, which had a small set of steps unseen from the street. The steps led directly to a small terrace on the roof. They climbed up and began walking across it, hunched down low.

As they were doing this, the police had already entered the second apartment on the ground floor, where a young European girl had been cleaning, letting them in with a surprised expression. After sweeping this apartment, they knew the target was the upper floor and decided to storm both flats simultaneously. They rang the doorbells and prepared to move in.

At this point, Oleg and Sabrina were working their way across the rooftops. They clambered over a series of small terraces, some covered with pots and plants and some empty. Oleg pointed to the planned exit. It was an old iron emergency exit spiralling down the side of the building. They started towards it.

Jussi waited with some officers outside one of the apartments. Some heavily armed officers had now arrived with what looked like machine guns.

You don't see much of this in Rauma, Jussi thought to himself.

There was no answer from either apartment, so battering

rams were employed to break open the doors.

Crash!

The noise was deafening in the stone stairwell as both doors gave in quickly. Shouts in both English and Chinese rang out, and there was a burst of activity. After a few moments, it was apparent that no one was in either apartment, as they searched all of the rooms.

"Here!" one of the officers shouted when he found the small balcony and stairs.

"Let's go!" the leading officer said to Jussi.

They filed up the stairs, following two of the heavily armed officers.

Oleg helped Sabrina down from the final rung, at the bottom of the fire escape, where it didn't quite reach the bottom. She leapt into his arms, and Oleg caught her. At that moment, they caught sight of the police making their way across the same route they'd just taken.

"Follow me," said Oleg calmly.

They quickly made their way across the small internal courtyard.

Jussi and the others had already spotted them. They were now running across the roof, with the leading officer talking continuously into his radio.

Outside, Wen was mobilising other officers to head to the other buildings, keeping the original address under guard, just in case. Now, police officers were clattering down the same spiral staircase: six of them.

Oleg was calmly aware of the noise in the background - now including sirens. He led Sabrina through a back gate and across a small park, where they walked towards a street filled with people. They made it to the road just as the police ran from all directions to the park. Jussi was entirely focused on the fugitives and ran with the small team, following them into the street. People scattered when they saw the guns.

Oleg heard the commotion behind them. He placed his hand into his pocket, where a Glock pistol nestled ready. They rounded another corner, and he hailed a taxi which came to a halt.

"Get out," he ordered the taxi driver, holding his handgun to the window.

The driver did so obediently and backed away. They got into the car, and Oleg pressed the accelerator, pulling away down the street. They turned into a wide boulevard, where he scanned for an exit ahead. The traffic lights turned green for them, not that Oleg would have waited. Then, they turned right. Slowing down, he drew into a small alley where he told Sabrina to get out of the car.

"Why are we leaving the car?" Sabrina asked.

"I always prefer to hide in plain sight. People always think that you'll run. So, I don't. Now, let's buy some new jackets and get a coffee over there."

Sabrina looked at him incredulously but did as she was told as they made their way to a small shopping centre.

Jussi was with another officer, talking to the abandoned taxi driver. They beckoned the team to follow them towards the boulevard. Within seconds, police cars arrived. As they did so, more officers cordoned off the surrounding area, stopping traffic and looking for the taxi in question.

Oleg ordered more coffee and began considering the lunch menu. Sabrina, although usually calm in a crisis, was trembling. She couldn't believe the situation had escalated so quickly and was worried about whether there was a way out.

Oleg made his choice and ordered the shrimp salad.

"Anything for you, Sabrina?" he asked calmly.

"No, thank you," she replied, her face firmly fixed on the exit.

Oleg ordered her the same thing anyway, if only for appearance's sake.

Jussi stood looking at the abandoned taxi. The couple had discarded it and continued on foot. He looked around and walked along the street with Wen and two of his officers. Other officers were checking trash collection areas and walking into office buildings.

"Jussi, will you walk ahead with us? No doubt you will recognise them if you see them." Wen asked.

Wen had read the file and was captivated by the story so far, especially by Jussi's involvement and tenacity with the case.

"With pleasure, Wen. If I see them, I'll recognise them immediately."

They continued to walk through the streets, occasionally walking into a shopping arcade, store or café. Noting a small shopping centre, Jussi walked up the steps and surveyed the area. All seemed normal. Wen followed him and gestured for the two officers to circulate. There seemed nothing untoward, so they turned to leave.

As they did so, Jussi suddenly found himself staring into a café - straight into Sabrina's eyes.

"There!" he shouted.

Oleg saw Jussi and sprang into action, grabbing Sabrina by the arm and walking her to the rear of the café. Kicking open what he thought was an exit, he almost threw her into the concrete passage, slamming the door shut with his foot. Oleg glanced around the space. There was no other door: it was a storeroom.

Now, the police were approaching the café with their guns drawn, yelling to everyone to get down onto the floor. The diners obliged, and Jussi approached the door. As he did so, Oleg decided there was only one option available. He smiled at Sabrina, grabbed the door handle, pointed his gun, opened the door and walked out shooting.

Although a crack shot, Oleg didn't stand a chance and was quickly brought down by a tirade of bullets from officers standing by the exit of the shopping centre. Everyone dived to the floor as they fired. Oleg crumpled to the ground.

Jussi shouted, "Sabrina, come out with your hands up!"

Sabrina decided this was also her only choice. She looked around quickly, and seeing a high shelf, threw the bag with the laptop onto it in the hope of later retrieval.

She walked out with her hands in the air and hatred in her eyes. Noticing Oleg, she dropped to the floor, just as he faded from the world - his eyes smiling at her one last time.

"No!" she yelled with anger.

Without thinking, she picked up the pistol and shot wildly in the direction of Jussi. Another volley of shots rang out, and she too fell to the floor.

They had been searching for the suspects a few moments before. After a brief sighting, they were both dead. Jussi was thankful that Heli was not with them. Still, his eyes searched the area, but it seemed she was absent.

He returned to Wen, who was surveying the scene, shaking his head.

"What a waste," Wen commented.

They looked at the body of the beautiful Sabrina, now lifeless and still.

Wen gave directions to his men, and the area was cordoned off. The police searched the area and soon returned with Sabrina's bag, recovered from the storage room. One officer, wearing gloves, carefully removed various items, including the laptop, which he showed to the team and returned to the bag. As the officers continued their work, Jussi, Wen and the officer with the bag walked to a waiting car and drove to the police station.

◆ ◆ ◆

Back at the station, Jussi sat in an office, nursing a cup of coffee. An empty sandwich wrapper was sat in front of him.

That was a good sandwich, he thought, *and well-needed.*

They had been very hospitable in Singapore, and everything seemed very efficient. He was impressed.

Wen opened the glass door and came in.

"We have accessed the laptop. There was quite some security but not enough for our people," he smiled.

Jussi smiled back expectantly.

"They've found references to several international bank accounts. It'll take a while, but we're confident that we'll be able to unravel the puzzle that leads to the money, or at least some of it."

"That's great. Let's leave it to the governments to discuss what happens next with that. Has there been any sign of the other member of the gang? The other female?" Jussi asked.

"No, I don't think she came to Singapore. Of course, we'll investigation further, but we've found no trace of her so far. What are your plans now, Jussi?" asked Wen.

"I think it's time for me to plan my return home."

"Already?" Wen asked disappointedly. "I think I can justify you being here for a couple of days to support us with the investigation and also to share some best practice. Besides, you must come for dinner. Please, I insist."

"Well, that sounds great. Thank you. Perhaps a quick freshen-up at the hotel first, though?"

"Yes, of course, you must be exhausted. I'll have someone drive you to your hotel and collect you in a few hours. Perhaps at 19.30?"

"Sounds perfect," Jussi replied.

Later, at his hotel, Jussi looked out of his window across the city. It was beginning to darken, and the city lights were coming to life in a spectacular fashion.

His hotel was downtown, and with his room being on a high floor, it commanded panoramic views. He marvelled at the incredible hotel across the water, with its dual towers and ship-shaped terrace at the top. He smiled and decided that he should definitely make time for a mojito at that particular bar.

BAD NEWS

Heli sat at the internet console as her fingers tapped instructions into the flight-finder website. She tutted to herself as she tested out various routes. She looked up for a second, sensing someone approaching, and minimized the screen as she did so. A waiter appeared and set down a napkin with an ice-cold glass of water.

"Thank you," she said in return and took a small sip.

Then, it was back to her task. She had decided that although she loved this island, it was time to move on. People were getting to know her too well. She felt that the hotel staff knew her habits, and if she was to remain anonymous, she needed a change of scene.

Heli had decided on Jamaica. It was not far away and had an equally hot and sunny climate. There was something about the place that had fascinated her for a long time. Bob Marley, jerk chicken and cocktails, all sounded good, and a month there would make a nice change. After that, she would return to St Lucia.

Heli scoured the list and made her selection of flight and hotel. She left the public console and returned to her room. She logged on again and paid for the trip using her new smartphone, which she had bought during one of her rare forays to the nearby town. She reminded herself to destroy the sim card before leaving Saint Lucia and purchase a new one on arrival in Kingston. She packed a few items of clothing that she had decided to take with her and left the other things for the maids. The rest of the day was spent lounging around the pool as she had arranged for a late checkout.

The taxi arrived at 4 pm and commenced the slow, one hour and a half journey to the airport. The car meandered around the hills as Heli took in the views.

Finally, they arrived at the airport. Heli had decided it was time to start enjoying her money and booked a business class seat. Having only one small terminal meant that she quickly went through the formalities and found herself in the business lounge.

Yes, It's time I started behaving like the millionairess I am.

The flight arrived on time, and she boarded the plane. She was soon settled with a glass of champagne as the evening flight took off into the sunset.

After the short flight to Kingston, Heli found herself walking through the terminal where a small shopping arcade caught her eye. She purchased new beachwear and a new phone. Pleased with her purchases, she made her way to the exit, got into a taxi and made her way to her chosen hotel in Negril.

On arrival at the hotel, she decided she was happy with her choice, as she viewed the long sandy beach laid out in front of her. Although there were more tourists here than her previous hotel, perhaps it was better that way. It was easier to blend in with a crowd rather than being the one everyone noticed.

When she arrived, a familiar pattern repeated itself. She was brought a rum cocktail, which she savoured while checking in. The receptionist was surprised when she announced she had no luggage to speak of. Heli replied that she preferred to travel light to get through airports quicker while on her tour of the Caribbean.

The following day, Heli swept into the open hotel lounge, aiming to take herself for a walk around the complex and orientate herself with its facilities. This hotel was less authentic than the one in Saint Lucia. However, it was much more luxurious.

She enjoyed a leisurely breakfast and spent most of the day moving between the beach and the enormous swimming pool, followed by a short nap.

Later, when Heli awoke, she felt hungry. She slipped on a light floral summer dress and made her way to the terrace. As she did so, she picked up a newspaper from a pile sitting on a teak table to take with her.

The evening was beautiful and Caribbean music floated around the grounds. Heli made her way towards the beach and sighed as she stood at the water's edge, watching the sunset for a moment; it seemed even more glorious here than in Saint Lucia. She couldn't resist slipping her sandals off and feeling the sand on her feet for a few moments. Then, she made her way to the small wooden restaurant by the beach and approached a podium, where a waiter was smiling in her direction.

"Do you have a table for one available?" she asked.

The waiter looked around, and although there were several people in the restaurant eating and more sitting at the bar, he ushered her to a prime table. It was just by the beach, with a beautiful view of the sunset.

"Thank you," she whispered.

She smiled coyly, and the waiter flashed a huge smile in return and retreated. He was back in a moment with a bright red drink, which he explained was the house cocktail for that evening. She took a sip and thanked him. It was intense, but she appreciated the taste of rum mixed with fresh fruit. To eat, she ordered some crispy prawns in batter, followed by jerk chicken with rice and peas and settled back in her chair.

She remembered the newspaper and opened it. There were the usual stories, but an article in the international news section particularly caught her eye. She read the article and couldn't believe its contents.

The story was about a criminal gang that had been discovered in Singapore. Multiple shootings had taken place. It read that two people had been found dead in a hotel suite and was suspected to be a deal gone bad. Two suspects had subsequently been found in a shopping centre. They had resisted arrest and were shot by police. She didn't recognize all of the names and places as she scanned the article. However, she immediately recognized two faces: Sabrina and Oleg.

"They're dead," she uttered under her breath in disbelief.

How could that happen? If there were two skilled criminals that walked the earth, it was those two, and here I am - alive and well.

Heli had read about Stanislav on her way to Denmark and now this. She was now the only one left. She started to ask herself if she was far enough away from danger? They had been in Singapore; wasn't that far enough away from Finland? What was Oleg doing there with her? Who were the other two men that had been shot? Were there more people looking for her?

Heli's mind was running so fast that it blocked out everything else.

"Excuse me, Miss? Miss?"

Her head rose from the newspaper as she was suddenly aware of the waiter talking to her.

"Oh, I'm sorry," she muttered, and sat back to give him space, hurridly folding the newspaper.

The waiter presented her with her first course and then reached over to pour a glass of white burgundy. She took a sip and nodded, attempting to smile.

The evening passed slowly, with her thoughts fixed firmly on the newspaper report. However, common sense told her that she was far away from Singapore, Sweden or Finland. She had flown to Saint Lucia, and now she was in Jamaica.

This place is remote enough. Probably the worst thing I could do right now is to panic. That's it. I should keep my cool and act as if nothing has happened.

She was here under a false passport. Nobody would know that name here, let alone her real name. The only thing that occurred to her was that as the hotel was such a high profile one, perhaps it would be more sensible to move to somewhere more remote? She could go somewhere where nobody could get to know her. Maybe she could rent a cottage?

At that point, the arrival of her main course interrupted her thoughts. She began to eat again. Really, she wasn't hungry at all, but Heli was telling herself that she should eat while she had the opportunity. She had gone into survival mode.

After eating enough, Heli downed a second glass of wine. She declined a dessert and left the table.

I need to get to my room, lock the door and get to work.

After a broken night's sleep, Heli awoke in the morning with the sun streaming in through the drapes. There had been a knock at the door, which had startled her.

She asked tentatively, "Hello, who's there?"

"Room service Ma'am, your breakfast."

Heli opened the door slowly and a young maid entered with an enormous silver tray. She had forgotten that she had arranged breakfast in bed.

"Thank you," she said.

Heli sat down in the living area by the French doors and poured herself a glass of fresh orange juice. She smiled half-heartedly as she looked at the impressive breakfast. This should have signified things to come, but maybe things would not be so easy now?

Heli tucked into the breakfast with an appetite that surprised her. She hadn't slept well during the night, so she was going to make up for it with calories.

Before long, Heli found herself on the way to downtown Kingston. She intended to visit an estate agent and discuss rental options. Her cover story was that she was a writer and wanted to spend some months researching and writing her new book.

At an agent's office, she went through various rental properties and settled on some potentials. The agent agreed with her choices, and they made their way to the agent's car to begin her viewing tour.

A long day followed because Heli hadn't appreciated the distances between the properties. However, she liked the remoteness of one of them. It was in the countryside but just close enough to walk to a village with a local store. She didn't want to rent a car as that would be too visible. She explained to the agent that she would pay in cash in advance, as she was very protective of her bank account, having been a victim of fraud in the past.

Once business was concluded, she returned to the hotel and packed her things. Having provided an excuse to the receptionist for why she was leaving early, she took a taxi to her new home, for at least the next three months.

On the way, she purchased some essentials, including food and drinks. She would have to get used to drinking rum in the absence of good wine, so she took a range of soft drinks and juices with which to mix it.

That evening, she stood on her terrace overlooking the trees. In the distance, she could just see the sparkling sea. Her hands cradled a glass of rum and mango juice. The future looked a little different now and she would have to be more careful. She was on the run again and this could be her life from now on. For now though, this was not a bad place to hide.

BECOMING CLEARER

Jussi returned to his hotel room after an entertaining evening. Wen had taken him to a street-food restaurant, which on face value hadn't looked that special. However, the owner had taken great delight in seeing Wen and lavished them with attentive service. Jussi could honestly say, and did so several times, that the food was some of the best he had tasted in his life. He enjoyed a wide range of dishes with a variety of exotic flavours, washed down with local ice-cold beer.

After dinner, he was taken to a small café for ice cream and espresso; the perfect ending to the meal. He had never been to a country like this and vowed he would return to explore it more deeply. Singapore seemed to have everything. He could see why Sabrina had moved here. From what he knew about her, it seemed the perfect place for her tastes.

During the dinner, Wen had revealed some new information: the two men found dead in the hotel room were a wealthy, international art dealer and his bodyguard.

"So, was there a transaction going on?" asked Jussi.

Wen replied, "Yes, we believe that certain artefacts had already been sold or were in the process of being, and somehow, something went wrong. I'm sure there is much more of this story yet to come to the surface. Let's see how it connects to your 'Paintings of Rauma' mystery."

Wen also asked about Heli. Everyone knew her name and her

movements now. There was quite a dossier building up around the whole case.

How long can she remain in hiding? Jussi wondered

Everything seemed to be closing in on her; the police were gradually unravelling mysteries all over the world. It was conceivable that if the other gang members were dead, that she could be too. He hated to think that and changed the subject of conversation as soon as it was polite to do so.

After the evening ended, Jussi returned to his hotel but was still restless, so he took himself for a walk. While he was walking, his phone buzzed with a new message, and he stopped for a moment by a small river and checked the content. His eyes widened.

Could this get any more mysterious?

The message from Wen explained that the Singaporean police had accessed the art dealer's laptop and found the items traded were precious artefacts. These had included a Fabergé Egg - worth tens of millions.

Jussi gasped.

No wonder the gang went to great lengths to find and protect their treasure.

The message concluded that there had been large transactions between the dealer, Sabrina and other gang members, assumed to be relevant to the precious items. The reason for the meeting at the hotel was unclear. Possibly there were additional items to be traded, or there was a problem with the original transaction. The financial investigation was ongoing.

Jussi shook his head. This kind of thing just didn't happen in Rauma. If someone had asked him a few months ago, if he expected to be in Singapore, chasing armed gang members who had stolen a Faberge egg, with almost everyone involved ending up dead - he would have laughed out loud.

He returned to his hotel, packed for the morning's flight and tried to sleep as best he could.

Jussi's return flight to Helsinki had been arranged for the following afternoon. This gave him time to catch up on the emails and documents circulating the different countries involved. Heli's name was being mentioned with greater frequency, and he was becoming more and more concerned. They had found that she had left Sweden and were checking different names to determine which one she was currently travelling under. If they found the correct name, they would be able to trace her whereabouts. Within some countries, she could be relatively easy to locate. They had already narrowed the search down to several possible places, including South America, the Caribbean and the United States. There was still a long way to go, though.

He decided to go for a walk before the flight and get some good food before he left. The area nearby was full of small street food places with people enjoying their lunch. He chose one such 'hawker centre', and ate some of Singapore's famous chicken noodles, washed down with a large coke.

Now he was ready for the flight home and returned to his hotel where he took a taxi and was soon waiting in the lounge at Changi airport. His long journey home, plus all of the waiting, was about to begin.

It would be almost twenty hours before he would find himself back home in Rauma once again.

MOVING ON

Jussi awoke at his house in Rauma and opened the blinds. The sun streamed in, which instinctively made him smile. Spring would be here soon, and the arrival of bright sunshine changed much about the world. He made himself a coffee and decided to dress and walk to the local café. He had missed his routine of visiting the café on the square for his favourite cappuccino.

He particularly enjoyed his coffee that morning. He chatted with the girl behind the counter and sat at his usual spot by the window. He was already aware that he was on his own again, and his mind frequently returned to thoughts of Heli.

His shift at work would start later that afternoon due to his long journey back from Singapore. He noted he had been allocated a short shift, which he appreciated. He had no doubt been given a gentle return to work due to his recent hectic schedule.

Before long, he found himself back at the Rauma Police Station and the butt of various jokes about his adventures and international travel - all well-meaning.

He spent some time in the inspector's office, debriefing Maarit and the others about the Singapore trip. There was new information coming in by the hour, and other pieces of information were shared back to him, some of which he had been unaware.

One particular snippet referred directly to Heli. She had been positively identified as travelling under the false passport of one

Susan Nordberg. She had travelled from Sweden to Denmark and flown onwards to Saint Lucia. They were currently working with the local police there to understand her movements.

Maarit had a quiet word with Jussi after the meeting. She had decided that he should read the complete file on the investigation, add any additional information, and then withdraw from the case. This was primarily due to his relationship with Heli. Nobody blamed him for anything, and his conduct had been exemplary throughout. Still, he could be compromised and would only be used in the continuing investigation if something specific required his input. Jussi hadn't protested, and he had not only agreed but expressed his wish to distance himself from the whole affair. In reality, he would prefer not to know what was happening to Heli. He would rest easy, just knowing she had disappeared somewhere safe.

At that moment, Heli was in a very different place and a very different state of mind. She had awoken late, as was her habit these days, tending to stay up and enjoy the warm evenings. She had decided to walk down to the beach and have a swim. After this, she walked to the small town to buy a few provisions and drink an ice-cold grapefruit soda. It was a perfect day, and she chatted briefly with the store owner. After which, she strolled back up the long hill.

On arrival, she poured herself a glass of cold water, picked up her iPad and flopped into her favourite basket chair. She was paying more attention to the news after the Singapore revelations and opened an international online newspaper to browse. Not seeing anything of any significance, she clicked on one of the local Jamaican news pages, which she had started to read. She was horrified to find a photograph of herself on one of the pages staring back at her.

The page announced: International Criminal thought to be in Jamaica. There followed quite a detailed background story, together with a profile of her. She didn't recognise herself in the description of a potentially dangerous international criminal. She stood up and looked around her hideaway. She felt relatively secure here, provided she stayed here as much as possible and only ventured out at night. She thought about her options as the day progressed, not daring to do anything away from the relative safety of the house.

Finally, she decided she would take a risk and visit a local supermarket for a few things. She would buy some hair dye and change her hairstyle. Also, she would buy some new clothes, sunglasses, make-up, scarves and other things, which would help change her identity as much as practical.

◆ ◆ ◆

Later that day, Heli found herself in a supermarket in Kingston. There had been nothing useful in the small local store, so with sunglasses and her hair swept forward, she had decided to take a risk and visit the capital.

She found the sights and sounds of Kingston enthralling, with the Caribbean beat of calypso ever-present wherever she went. There were plenty of people around, and Heli felt able to blend in easily.

She visited the supermarket and selected some necessities. Next, she meandered down the street and picked up a few pieces of clothing: a wide-brimmed hat was perfect plus a couple of silk scarves and some new pairs of sunglasses.

It was thirty-two degrees, and after a while, shopping had started to wear her down. Walking by some souvenir stores, she picked up some street food and stood at a tall cocktail table munching on a jerk chicken sandwich and drinking a small cold beer. As she stood there, she noticed some men taking an interest in her at the opposite side of the alley.

Time to move, she decided.

Although she was accustomed to attracting men's attention from time to time, she didn't want to be noticed anywhere at the moment. She took a large drink from her cup, tossed the remainder of her sandwich into the trash can and walked straight to the nearest taxi rank.

"To Harmony, please," she asked the driver.

Harmony being a nearby town and part of her elaborate routine to avoid being tracked.

"Iree, just relax, and I'll have you there in no time at all," replied the driver.

She sat reading her phone on the way back, not wishing to engage the driver in conversation.

On arrival, she wandered around for a few minutes and then caught another taxi to the small village nearest her house.

At the village, she walked back up the hill to her place. It was with some relief that she arrived at the house. She gasped an audible sigh of relief in her hallway.

After placing her provisions in the fridge, she went straight to the bathroom and began dying her hair. As she massaged the dye into her hair, it became darker, almost black. Then, she cut it shorter, combing it to one side with strong gel and hairspray. She threw away her old lipstick and tested out a new colour. Approving the change, she fixed herself a rum and coke and went out onto the rear terrace to her preferred spot.

"Whatever am I going to do?" she asked a toucan sitting in some nearby trees, which tilted its head with a puzzled expression.

Currently, the best option seemed to be to stay put and maintain a low profile. Heli couldn't imagine the Jamaican police force conducting house to house searches across the whole island. The only risk would be when she needed to go somewhere, but perhaps the publicity would have died down by then? She would be yesterday's news soon enough and long forgotten. Not totally convincing herself, she decided to occupy herself looking for alternative ways to leave the island.

On her tablet computer, she researched different day trips to places as possible escape routes. She was improving in her role as a criminal on the run.

Back in Finland, Jussi sighed as he watched a car drive past their speed control point. They were back at one of their usual places to catch speeding motorists, with the spring sun gearing drivers into a faster driving mode. Pekka accompanied him that day. He looked sideways at Jussi with a concerned expression.

"That was some sigh, Jussi. Is traffic duty getting you down after international crime-busting?"

Jussi cast a disparaging look in his direction.

"No, on the contrary, it's nice to be back doing something normal again, instead of people shooting at each other."

Pekka tilted his head a little.

"Are you sure?"

"Well, kind of. I can't get the whole thing out of my head. Heli really misled me. I thought she was so genuine," he replied.

"Well, part of it could've been, but she also had another plan. Money can change people, you know?"

Jussi nodded and raised the speed gun at an approaching driver. Noting the figure, he opened the car door to flag them down.

"Off we go again," he said.

SEPARATE WAYS

Time passed, and Heli's house rental tenancy was nearing its end. She had been correct in thinking that everything about her and the newspaper story would soon die down sufficiently for her to feel safe again. However, she still couldn't risk leaving the island by any public form of transport, if at all. Also, she was starting to feel as if she couldn't exist here for much longer. She was on her own, with no company and little to occupy herself.

She sat down after a light lunch one day and started to make decisions. There weren't too many viable options. She made a list: Stay here and renew the lease, locate another place on the island, or leave quietly. She found a good possibility for the last option: a boat skipper willing to make the long trip to Cuba. This would enable her to leave Jamaica quietly and arrive on her false passport for a Cuban vacation. She could stay there for a month, with the possibility of extending that time, if she could find a good reason. From there, she could transfer to somewhere like the Caymans, using a similar method.

After much deliberation, the decision was made: it was time to leave Jamaica. She called the skipper in question, who made occasional tourist trips with his fishing boat and arranged a private excursion. It was a considerable distance, and the fisherman wanted $1000, but she was happy to pay it. Besides, she had probably made more money in bank interest than she had spent over the past month or so.

Early the following day, she left a note together with a generous tip for the cleaner. She packed her bag and dumped the rest of her Jamaican life in the trash.

She walked to the small village, where she repeated her double-taxi routine so as not to raise suspicion. She arrived at the pier just before 6 am. The fisherman came slightly late, much to her annoyance but then waved her on board, started the engines, and cast off.

The journey was interminable. Even though the boat was fast and the sea and wind kind to it, the trip took almost fourteen hours. Heli didn't feel good on the voyage either. She had no problem with boats but had never been aboard one for that long. She was extremely relieved to see Santiago de Cuba appear on the horizon.

On arrival, they docked and completed immigration. The fisherman would stay on board and leave the following day with the tide. Heli would find her hotel, which she had pre-booked for two weeks, wishing to appear like a tourist, and decide what to do from thereon.

She had selected a small hotel near Varahicacos nature reserve. It offered all the usual amenities without being too expensive. It was also the type of place where she could remain unnoticed.

As soon as she arrived, she felt more comfortable. She had discovered that Cuba was out of reach of any extradition treaties, and international law wouldn't be able to reach her here. In addition, she had always wanted to visit Cuba and felt she could finally be herself here. She was looking forward to exploring this fascinating country.

It wasn't long after her arrival that she was eating and drinking at the resort and enjoying a live band playing Cuba's unique brand of Rumba. She started to wonder if this place could become her new home.

The international task force, set up after the events in Stockholm and Singapore, had amassed alot of information. They had almost the entire sequence of events mapped out and had already traced much of the money through the recovered laptops. They had also located the Fabergé egg and many other items of dubious sources from the art dealers' home in Nyon, Switzerland. The list of charges was considerable, although the majority of them had been applied posthumously as non-pursuant. However, many could still be charged to the sole-surviving member of the gang.

They had traced Heli's journey across a large map on the wall, but as yet, principally due to its small police force, they hadn't found her whereabouts in Jamaica. Therefore, Interpol representatives flew to the island and were currently working with local authorities on possible leads to her location. Unbeknown to them, Heli was already in Cuba, drinking in her first taste of the country.

Through investigations with Jamaican estate agents, it wasn't long before the police located the house that Heli had rented. A search commenced for her in other hotels, guest houses and independent rentals across the island.

After two weeks, they drew a blank but then hit a lucky strike when they checked the routes by vessels leaving Montego Bay and interviewed the skippers. It wasn't long afterwards that they came across a solitary fisherman who explained all: Heli was now known to be in Cuba. They immediately started a chain of communication with the authorities there, but it was unlikely to lead anywhere. Cuba had its own rules, and they may have to wait until she left.

A few days later, Jussi heard some news from the Inspector, who brought him into the office. Maarit told him they knew she had travelled to Cuba, but that was the last thing they had heard. Police investigations were not allowed to continue there. So, they had alerted the United States and other countries, hoping her passport might flag up in the future.

Jussi was quietly relieved to hear that Heli had escaped. However, she was still missing, and he was still concerned.

Had made Cuba her home? Left the island undetected? Or had some mishap had befallen her?

Nobody knew.

Some months later, a lady with long blonde hair and green eyes was standing at a bar in downtown Havana, talking to an American who asked her name.

"Heli." she said, "My name is Heli," with a big smile and a Finnish accent.

She had a feeling that she had finally found her safe haven.

The story didn't reach Jussi. However, he had already convinced himself that she was happy and living in Cuba. This enabled him to find the comfort he needed and toast her good fortune for the final time.

Jussi strolled down Kuninkaankatu, glancing at the usual stores. The temperature was rising now, and the days were getting longer; summer was finally coming to Rauma.

Things were changing for him as well. Thanks to the case of

'The Paintings of Rauma', a job in Helsinki now beckoned. His ambition to be a detective was soon to be realised and he would begin his training in two weeks; no doubt an exciting career lay ahead.

Jussi smiled to himself and quickened his pace as he strode across the town square, towards home.

What adventures will Helsinki bring? he wondered.

The End

ABOUT THE AUTHOR

John Swallow

I'm originally from Yorkshire, England and have been fortunate to have also lived in countries as diverse as Scotland, Argentina, Latvia and now Finland.

I enjoy writing crime adventures and about the supernatural. The common factor in my stories is that they are usually based in Finland and often in my adopted home town of Rauma.

Thank you for reading my book. If you wish, you can follow my writing at: https://raumastories.blogspot.com

And if you a few moments to spare, a short review would be greatly appreciated on Amazon or Goodreads. Thank you!

I hope you enjoyed reading this novel as much as I enjoyed writing it!

THE JUSSI ALONEN DETECTIVE ADVENTURES

Jussi Alonen is a Police Officer, based in Rauma, Finland. His career takes him towards his ambition of being a detective and beyond.

From being based in Rauma and then Helsinki, his journey takes him on a series of exciting adventures to many different countries. Follow Jussi across Finland, the Åland Islands, Sweden, Singapore, Latvia, Russia and more.

His challenges include theft, murder and organised crime. In addition, his romantic interludes give him just as much cause to struggle.

Follow Jussi's adventures in "The Paintings of Rauma" and "The Waves of Helsinki" and join Jussi Alonen for a taste of Finland's Nordic Noir.

The Paintings Of Rauma

The Paintings of Rauma takes the reader to Finland for a thrilling crime adventure. The story is based in the beautiful coastal city of Rauma and takes Jussi Alonen, a local Police Officer, on a journey to investigate connected crimes across Finland, Sweden and Singapore.

This Nordic Noir mystery begins with a minor incident that sets in motion a chain of events involving theft, murder, passion and hidden treasure.

Jussi's life is turned upside down when someone from the past comes back into his life. A gang of criminals make their way around Finland, wreaking havoc in search of great wealth. Treasure from the past is found and millions are made and then lost.

Jussi discovers there is much more to police work in Rauma than he could ever imagine.

The Waves Of Helsinki

The Waves of Helsinki takes the reader back to Finland for a thrilling new crime adventure. This time, the story is based in Helsinki, the spectacular capital city of Finland.

Jussi Alonen is now training to be a detective and becomes involved in an intriguing investigation which quickly escalates.

This Nordic Noir mystery begins with some apparently small thefts, which if not stopped, will escalate to the spread of major organised crime.

Jussi's career is heading towards his ambition of being a fully-fledged detective, that's if he can survive the events in Helsinki, Latvia, Russia and his home town of Rauma.

Theft and murder on the high seas, combined with a new romance, will challenge Jussi more than he ever thought possible.

The Heat Of Havana

The Heat of Havana finds Detective Jussi Alonen settled down in Rauma once again. However, little does he know that a thrilling new adventure awaits him, one which will not only reconnect him with an old flame but also result in his involvement with international crime once again.

Smuggling high-quality Cuban cigars to wealthy Eastern Europeans is a lucrative business. However, when a problem arises, Jussi's old friend Heli finds herself in the wrong place at the wrong time and he unexpectedly finds himself in Havana. Can he save her and return to his life as a detective in Finland?

This Nordic Noir mystery gradually evolves into high-octane action as Jussi's new nemesis follows him from Cuba to Finland, with both bent on revenge, in this gripping new story.

Cigars, mojitos and rumba turn into kidnapping, smuggling and murder, immersing Jussi in his most exciting adventure yet!